John Milton, Ernest Myers

Selected prose writings. With an introductory essay by Ernest Myers

John Milton, Ernest Myers

Selected prose writings. With an introductory essay by Ernest Myers

ISBN/EAN: 9783337282110

Printed in Europe, USA, Canada, Australia, Japan

Cover: Foto ©Andreas Hilbeck / pixelio.de

More available books at **www.hansebooks.com**

SELECTED PROSE WRITINGS

OF

OHN MILTON

WITH AN INTRODUCTORY ESSAY

BY

ERNEST MYERS

NEW YORK

D. APPLETON AND COMPANY

1, 3, AND 5 BOND STREET

MDCCCLXXXIV

CONTENTS.

INTRODUCTION

SEVERAL English poets have written good prose, but Milton's alone has preserved any considerable power. Even his would have been forgotten but for its relation to his poetry. Much of his poetry was directly or indirectly affected by his interest in public affairs, and his prose works are the explicit expression of that interest. Many indeed of his arguments, and some of his conclusions, are such as can now have small hold on the minds of men. It is a certain spirit breathing through these pamphlets, and their style when it fitly expresses this spirit, that can still interest us; and thus may be justified the extraction of characteristic passages from what were of course intended in the first place to be persuasive chains of reasoning. Passages of imaginative eloquence are as subordinate to the argument in Milton as in Demosthenes, though they affect us very differently in the two writers, because, apart from his somewhat ineffective efforts to influence the changes proceeding in the state, Milton was primarily and ultimately a poet.

He turned from poetry to write pamphlets on political and ecclesiastical matters because he lived in a time of revolution, and with the main elements of that revolution he warmly sympathized. But how far can the forces then at work be said to have found expression in his writings? He tells us that the principle for which he strove was the threefold principle of civil, domestic, and religious liberty. This is hardly the principle avowed by the leaders of the Parliaments of 1628 and 1629, or even of the Long Parliament. Until the Independents became a power, Presbyterianism represented Puritanism, and was more intolerant than Anglicanism. In the Grand Remonstrance it is the suppression of innovations that is spoken of as the object of the address. In Church matters the Parliament 'hold it requisite 'that there should be throughout the whole realm 'conformity to that order which the laws enjoin 'according to the word of God.' Though it was barely a century since the establishment of the Reformation in England, most Englishmen looked on returns to 'Popish practices' as innovations, and Parliament appealed to the conservative feeling of the English race against these, without misgiving as to the need of innovating to other purposes. Milton's 'Areopagitica,' written in 1644, is a demand for liberty for innovations to approve themselves if they can, though he too always regarded the Roman Church as rendering exceptional precautions needful.

Apart from the relief of physical hardship, the bulk of the people are only then strongly interested in political liberties and in exercising control of the

administration when they feel these indispensable
to the satisfaction of aspirations toward things that
touch them more nearly than constitutional abstractions. The English had been accustomed to leave administration to the Tudor princes, and even statesmen had then been willing to allow the crown unpre-
cedented power in order to curb the aggressions of
the nobles and of the Roman See. At the end of
Elizabeth's reign England was content, and no one
could have foreseen the coming troubles. It was
to be expected indeed that the crown, whoever
might be its wearer, would not easily be deprived
of the exceptional power which had been entrusted
to it for exceptional purposes ; it was to be expected
also that prescient men of affairs should see the
necessity of such deprivation, and should strive to
effect it. But they would not have got the majority
of the people to support them to the extent of
waging resolute and bloody civil war, had not more
been involved than political questions, even though
the political questions included illegal taxation.
The people rose in arms because they were con-
scious, more or less distinctly, of a great national
expansion and development, not in constitutional
politics but in spiritual and intellectual life, a
development which had produced the Shaksperian
stage as well as the Puritan pulpit. The one
essential thing for an English king to do who wished
to preserve his power, was to find some way of
identifying himself with this expansive movement,
as Elizabeth had done. A wise and large-minded

king might by this means have successfully maintained the Tudor type of monarchy against Eliot and Pym and Hampden and the minority who were statesmen enough to see the danger of the excessive power of the crown. But the Stuarts were, as we know, by no means wise or large-minded, and instead of identifying themselves in any way with the expansion they tried to stifle it exactly on that side where for the time it was strongest—the side of Puritanism. Puritanism was by no means the only side of it, nor the most likely to gain a permanent hold on the country. The average Englishman has little sympathy with Puritanism; he is fond of sport and good cheer, and does not care to follow a minority, however strenuous, which seems likely to take these from him. His own Reformation indeed was a comparatively easy-going affair, though not without its martyrdoms. But after the defeat of the Armada, England was far too full of receptive and active life to isolate herself from the waves of religious passion which were sweeping over Europe. The first half of the seventeenth century was the age of the Thirty Years' War. No Protestant country could help feeling her Protestantism intensified at such a time. Hence came the strength of Puritanism. If time had been given it, Puritanism would have subsided quietly within the natural limits assigned to it by the character of the English people. But the Stuarts and their bishops tried to dam the river, with what consequence we know.

Furthermore, the instrument with which this

attempt of the Stuart government was made was one by its nature singularly unsuited to the enforcement of any violent restriction, the Established Church of England. Not only had it none of the awful far-reaching traditions which might be put forward to excuse the Church of the Holy Roman Empire, the Church of the Crusaders, in employing the secular arm against heretics, as against traitors to militant Christendom ; but also its position at all times must be such as renders any forcible imposition of its claims unbefitting and perilous. The sects may gain by attacking it, it can only lose by attacking them. However active in its own work, it has to avoid aggression and even proselytizing. Its strength is to sit still, to cherish its best elements, and to trust that its tolerant eclecticism, its noble offices and chaste ritual, its scholarly traditions, may win over to it those whose desire for religious rest has been wearied or outraged by the exaggerations of other forms of Christianity. When it forsook the spirit of Hooker for that of Laud it made a false step which could only lead to painful defeat. Presbyterianism, with still less excuse, made a like aggression, and with like result.

To a certain extent therefore Milton is the spokesman of the bulk of his countrymen. Priest and Presbyter alike he forbade in the name of England to fetter by force her free development, her realization of her chosen ideals for the time being. But his own ideals were naturally such as the bulk of his countrymen could hardly as yet comprehend, much less adopt. Of his controversial pamphlets those on Church matters come the nearest to expressing popular feeling. But Milton's dislike of prelatical episcopacy was based on broader grounds than a dread of the return of Papist abuses. He rejoiced without scruple in the charm of the storied windows and pealing organ, the service high and anthem clear; for these he had only admiration and love. But he abhorred that association of worldly rank and wealth with spiritual functions which seemed to be involved in an established episcopal church. The taint of gain sullied religion as much as the taint of force.

Further still removed from popular ideas were his pamphlets on 'domestic' liberty, especially on liberty of divorce. Here also aspiration toward a high ideal was the motive of his contention. His ideal of true and perfect marriage seemed to him so sacred that he could not admit that considerations of expediency might justify the law in maintaining immutable any meaner kind, or at least any kind in which the vital element of spiritual harmony was not.

Nor does he stand much less by himself in his judgment of civil liberty. He is equally contemptuous of kings and of mobs, and partly for the same reasons. Both fail to offer the security of virtue and wisdom approved by adequate tests, both are eminently subject to narrow selfishness, to fear, and to the love of flattery. Shakspere has somewhat of this contempt for the populace, though

tempered by the tolerance of a great dramatic poet,
tolerance born of wide sympathetic insight, and
counting no human society wholly common or
unclean.   He would hardly have spoken as Milton
speaks of the average unaspiring lives of the majority:

> Nor do I name of men the common rout
> That wandering loose about
> Grow up and perish as the summer fly,
> Heads without name, no more rememberēd.

Shakspere expresses no dislike of hereditary
kings, though he measures them unsparingly by
their efficiency, and puts his assertion of the mystic
sanctity of coronation into the mouth of a king of
words not deeds, Richard II.   But to Milton the
extravagant exaltation of an accidental ruler, and
all the falseness and sickly atmosphere of a court,
seemed a defilement of the sacred trust of magistracy.
What he desired, as all profess to desire, was an
aristocracy in the literal sense, a rule of the best
and wisest, and he was not democratic enough to
expect to obtain these by unqualified popular
election.   In his 'Ready and Easy Way to Establish
'a Free Commonwealth' he proposes to have a
Grand Council sitting in permanent rule, and does
not hesitate to refer to the Venetian constitution
as in many points a worthy model.

The ultimate object of all political and social
machinery is, in his view, to allow and foster the
development of noble personalities, linked by all
possible social charities, yet preserving the individuality so much cherished by his countrymen.   He

saw the essential importance of mental training, drawn in great part from Hellenic and Italian sources, to enlarge and refine the sturdy insular stock from which he sprang himself. His Tract on Education deals with only the most complete kind of education, such as not more than a minority could have leisure to enjoy. Perhaps no man has done more than Milton to express the spirit which informs the peculiarly English word *gentleman,* with its indefinable standard of conduct and manners, of καλοκαγαθία, and its half jealous main-tenance half generous contempt of caste, allowing no stamp of birth or circumstances to guarantee the base metal, yet cautious in overlooking the absence of such stamp upon the true. It is from this position that Milton can despise the imposing pomps of monarchy and prelacy, not only as Knox or Luther might, by opposing greater and deeper things in another kind, but by competent estimate of them in their own kind with regard to their own aims. It is the consciousness of seeing more widely as well as of aiming higher than those about him concerned with the questions of the hour, that gives him his peculiar note of lofty pride, which becomes loftier the more arrogant the pretensions it confronts, as it were Zephon opposing Lucifer. So high and in some cases so isolated a pride might perhaps have been expected to repel us, yet instead of that our sympathy is attracted and we allow with enthusiasm his amplest claims. This is partly because, with all his independence and pre-eminence of intellect, he is not anxious to claim originality. As the Long Parliament had appealed to historic precedents, so Milton

> did but prompt the age to quit their clogs
> Ly the known rules of ancient liberty.

This suits the English character ; it loves indeed to cherish individuality, yet so that while each man shall do his work in his own way he shall endeavour to approve it by the sanction of some tradition, and by the mutual confidence inspired by recognition of a common thought and hope. Milton is as much greater than M. Renan as Dante than Politian, but we cannot imagine Milton announcing, as M. Renan announces of himself, that he was the first person to understand Jesus. And further, it is everywhere apparent that Milton had the most generous faith in the mind as well as in the heart of man, that whenever he felt others fall short of some intellectual or moral level he had himself attained, he not only longed but believed that they might rise to it, and moreover might so rise only as a small step in the ascent to a far higher state, toward which his whole life was an aspiration.

An ideal perfection of man—a perfection developed through trial—was indeed constantly in his mind, and partly influenced his choice of the subjects of his great poems. Mythological beliefs show the double tendency in man to imagine a golden age alike in the distant past and in the distant future. Of this Milton avails himself when

2

he accepts the doctrine of the Fall and Redemption as the central conception of his double epic; and thus obtains an idea of progress and development in human and even in divine history; for the Son of God himself is represented as realizing a higher perfection by his victory over the Tempter and by his accomplished self-sacrifice for the realization of justice and mercy. In this idea Milton stands almost alone even among poets; Æschylus, Shelley, and Tennyson seem most nearly to approach him. Shakspere is absorbed in the presentation of the world as it is, without comparing it with past or future; his historical plays are concerned with character, individual or national, not with historical progress or causation. Milton's idea of the perfectibility of man was connected with his vivid conception both of God as the transcendent perfection of humanity, and of human thought and will as inspired from the divine. Thus he makes Man the central person of a drama of the action of Gods, involving the mightiest powers of Heaven and Hell. The tragic interest would have been greater if Milton could have found some way of accepting a dualistic theory of the universe, in which the greater majesty and might of the Power of Good might have rested solely on virtue and wisdom, not also on a predestining omnipotence. Yet there is no easy optimism in him, such as would destroy the tragic solemnity of the enacted drama: only by painful struggle and after loss and suffering is the good victorious. The failure, or rather eclipse, in his beloved country of the cause for which he strove, was enough to leave this tone in every voice of his old age. It is the cruel waste, or seeming waste, of his labour, his eyesight, and his hope, in a great cause, which makes his personal utterances in his later poems so unspeakably pathetic, and heroic none the less. We seem to hear Prometheus on Caucasus, or Elijah on Horeb, or Milton's own Abdiel or Samson, left alone among the enemies of God.

It is to complete our conception of Milton's life and work and genius that some acquaintance with his prose works is needful; we may say also that without some such conception already derived from his poems we should hardly have read his prose. In the first place, prose is uncongenial to him; as he says of himself, he has here but the use of his left hand. This is not to be explained merely by saying that English prose was as yet hardly created, for after Bacon and Hooker, Milton might surely have hewn out a more perfect style for himself (as indeed now and again he does) if his heart had been in the work of writing prose as it was in the work of writing poetry. It is not so much that he uses his left hand as that he is encumbered with ill-fitting armour, fettering the wings which his proper celestial panoply would have left free. The art indeed of the best prose can be but as the art of clear and beautiful manuscript, enriched, it may be, by illuminations; the form is rather subordinate to the matter than incorporate with it; whereas poetry is more nearly (though by no means strictly) analogous to painting and sculpture, and the form and subject-matter are coördinate and mutually incorporate. Small indeed is the residue of prose from any pen that can be fully enjoyed two centuries, or even one, after it is written; prose is for an age, poetry for all time. But it is not merely the form, it is the matter of Milton's prose-writings that is in a sense uncongenial to him. The objects indeed for which he writes are objects deemed by him to be of the utmost importance. But they are of importance as needful but rudimentary preliminaries to the fulfilment of his true vocation. It is as though the architect of a Doric temple were compelled with his own hands wielding axe and spade to clear and level the ground for his building. Milton has to be his own forerunner, striving to prepare a highway in the wilderness. His absorbing passion was for beauty and virtue, his mission was to write poetry enshrining them, but he considered that for this end he was bound not only to 'make his life 'a poem,' that is, to develope it so far as he could toward his ideal, but also to do his best to free the society in which he lived from burdens and bondage fatal to its like development. Akin to Dante rather than to Goethe or even Shakspere, he was bent on realizing beauty in practical as well as contemplative, social as well as artistic life, in the state as well as in the individual. Resolutely as he contended in his pamphlets for liberty, he feels throughout a generous impatience of the task laid on him, an impatience leading him sometimes into utterance entangled by the rush of thoughts too obvious to himself to induce him to use much art in their arrangement, sometimes more deplorably, as it were in a kind of maddened weariness, into retorting the ferocious bitterness of the controversialists of his day. It is when he gives us glimpses of the ideal with which he contrasts the deformities he has been struggling against with his uncouth armoury of biblical texts and learned precedents—it is then that his style both clears itself and rises into something worthy of his poetry in artistic power. But these passages, noble and exalting as they are, make us feel, if they are anywhere prolonged, that they need both the limitations and the liberty of verse.

In the Abbey Church of Tewkesbury are still heard the tones of the very organ on which Milton played before Cromwell at Hampton Court ; and the picture thus evoked from the past symbolizes the true influence of poets such as Dante and Milton on the conduct of a commonwealth. But if they live, as these did, amidst 'a troubled sea of noises 'and harsh disputes,' such influence will not be felt till they are dead. It was, after all, well for Milton's work and fame that all hope of national regeneration in his lifetime was taken away at the recall of the Stuart dynasty. The tide of life swept away from the blind champion of liberty, leaving him still and solitary as a heroic statue among the drifted sands of the desert. But it was then that the holy Light arose upon him, and called forth his undying strain.

‘Milton, thou shouldst be living at this hour!’ Such is Wordsworth’s invocation to the man then more than a century dead, now more than two centuries; and I know not if any other poet has been invoked in like manner. We think of poets mostly as of men whose work was done once for all in leaving us the monuments of their art. That this poet should present himself differently to a reverer’s mind points to some distinguishing quality in Milton. It is the quality of strenuous desire to help to create around him a condition of things approaching and helping on the fulfilment of his poetic ideal. That was a gigantic task, and the rough struggle involved was fitter for a giant than for a seraph. Yet though his wings were tarnished they regained a tenfold lustre. They would doubtless regain it once more if he had been plunged in our conflicts of to-day. But it is better that they be not recalled to earthly soilure; he speaks to us in his works, and it is enough.

Indeed we may almost doubt further whether his would be the most appropriate healing voice at this hour. Each age has its own especial task, or rather some especial shape in which is presented the one perpetual task of developing for the best the physical, intellectual, and moral capacities of man. The lot of the seventeenth century was mainly to assert liberty, that of the nineteenth to assert fraternity. When the enslavers had been struck

down, would Milton have felt enough sympathy
with those who still remained enslaved by their own
ignorance or grossness to have made him brook the
wearisome toil of raising them? The Catholicism he
helped to banish for ever from dominion in England
spoke to the populace in more potent tones than
are possible to aristocratic, individualistic Protestantism. Eclectic Anglicanism repudiates the tinsel
of Rome as Milton did, but cannot find a substitute
for its attraction. The humanizing influence of
Catholicism was replaced in England by a philanthropy which grew up as much outside Churches as
within them. The growth of this new and wide
philanthropy became, not less than the growth
of physical science, a chief achievement of the
eighteenth century, so often reproached, and in
many ways justly, with materialism and corruption.
Politics had lost the idealizing influences of the
Puritan Revolution. Literature seemed to be
engrossed in forming a prose style. Gray, the
best poet born in England between the birth of
Milton and the birth of Wordsworth, was half
stifled by the insensibility of the age. Johnson's
comparison of the sonnets of Milton to imperfectly
carved cherry-stones marks the lowest point imaginable in criticism of verse. Yet from about this
point a revival in poetry begins, a return to nature,
in the van of which came Cowper, though with
somewhat uncertain steps. Nor is verse the only
vehicle of poetic thought. This was the age of
the rise of modern music, the age also of the most

famous English school of painting. If music be an
art too much apart to argue from, painting at least
may interpret somewhat of the spirit of a time.
Perhaps no work of Milton so characteristically
represents him, and through him the embattled
seventeenth century, as does his 'Samson Agonistes.'
If I were to choose one representative work of
English art of the eighteenth century to set over
against the 'Samson,' I would take Gainsborough's
masterpiece, 'The Girl with the Pitcher.'[1] A child
in ragged clothes stands in the foreground of a wood-
land landscape of undulating English green. Even
Reynolds' high-bred children are less exquisite
than this lovely one; the very soul of childhood
is in her divine simplicity and grace. Her rags
tell of painful poverty; but these give only one
touch in many by which the painter's genius has
made this one of the most pathetic as well as of the
most beautiful pictures in the world. The beauty
of sky, grass, and trees, the beauty of childhood,
are interfused with a magic tenderness in which
the world seems born anew and the pride of
human strength broken down. Before Gainsborough died England was beginning to find again
her natural voice of poetry, and only now again
after another century does that voice show signs of
failing her. But neither Wordsworth nor Shelley
nor Tennyson have spoken more magically to the
heart than that great painter of a prosaic age. In

---

[1] In Lord Coventry's collection.

passing from Milton's archangels to Wordsworth's peasants, poetry had been brought down, as philosophy by Socrates, from heaven to earth; but the kingdom of heaven is in both. Man was not to climb the firmament, but a great sheet was let down thence to him with the mysterious bidding: 'What God hath cleansed, that call not thou com- 'mon.' Perhaps we may be again entering on a prosaic age, though through somewhat different causes. In the eighteenth century there was doubtless a reaction after the failure of ideal aspirations. Now there is a depression from the growing sense of certain realities which seem to mar all hope of fulfilled ideals—chiefly the relentless struggle pervading Nature, and the grim contrasts of wasted wealth and wasting poverty. Even those who are remote from both these, and enjoy a life worthy of free men, may seem to themselves to be raised to the capacity of such life by standing on a heap of crushed human bodies, victims of the material civilization which must be in some degree the basis of intellectual. Milton knew little of this oppressing pity; if he were 'living at this hour' he would perhaps feel in bitter truth that 'an age 'too late' did at last indeed 'damp his intending 'wing.'

Yet, after all, Wordsworth's regretful cry might be in a manner justified even now, for our sake if not for Milton's. If there is any master-key to the perplexities of humanity, it will be ultimately revealed in some form or other by that 'plain heroic 'magnitude of mind' which colours with its glow all Milton's pictures of his ideal, an atmosphere in which materialism and its brood of evils cannot breathe. Even as the chief progress of ethical philosophy has confessedly been to enlarge the area of sympathies giving play to virtues essentially the same as those recognized by the reflective thought of ancient Hellas, so Milton's spirit, were he among us, might adapt itself to the conditions of our world, and find some means to 'give us 'manners, virtue, freedom, power.' In an age which bestows much of its applause, as well as its material rewards, on a restless mechanic industry, he might show that a meditative life is not inconsistent with active service of the commonwealth when occasion calls. In this, as in many other points, he is the English parallel to Dante, and his genius, like Dante's, while it suffered thereby in some ways, yet gained in others. And whereas Dante could only soften the bitterness of his discouragement in the air of a far-off supernatural world of the redeemed, Milton attained to a steadfast hope, embracing earth as well as heaven in a gaze profoundly saddened but not despairing or unbenign. If we look from him to his twin pillar of the imperishable temple of English poetry, his relation to Shakspere can hardly be more aptly expressed than by the familiar lines :

> For there was Milton like a seraph strong,
> Beside him Shakspere bland and mild.

Yet, for all Shakspere's large benignity, his farewell

words that speak of the dissolution of the world and 'all which it inherit,' though fully as majestic and resigned, have less of forward-looking hope in them than Milton's last utterance over the slain Samson, the chorus still rejoicing in

> new acquist
> Of true experience from this great event.

Milton had battled for the aspirations and against the basenesses of man; Shakspere had comprehended both, but it was not his to strive or cry. He is our greatest, and has taught us most; yet we feel that to call on him as Wordsworth calls on Milton would strike a jarring and ineffectual note. So far as we can know his personality at all, it is that of one who, much as he loved his fellow-men, deemed that he had played out his part among them. His work is done once for all, in many parts with obvious imperfections, yet as a whole producing an impression of universality resembling rather the abiding presence of Nature herself than any human personality whose law is to learn and to progress. His mild and magic rays are poured over the whole earthly scene with divine impartiality, over the castle and the cottage, the battle-field and the village-green, the wild sea hurled against the cliff, and the still river winding through the plain. Looking thence to the genius of Milton we seem to see a pillar of clear fire mingled with smoke, throwing back strong shadows on the spurned earth, as it towers indignantly away. But if we follow it with unblenching eyes we find it grow purer and softer in its ascent, until within the empyrean it blends with the holy Light hailed by the old man in his blind solitude, the same light that bathed Dante when he felt his will moved with the sun and stars, the light of love, the one source and soul of joy.

OF REFORMATION IN ENGLAND

AND THE CAUSES THAT HITHERTO
HAVE HINDERED IT. IN TWO BOOKS
WRITTEN TO A FRIEND. 1641.

The two following specimens are from the beginning of the First and from the end of the Second Books respectively.

SIR,—Amidst those deep and retired thoughts, which, with every man Christianly instructed, ought to be most frequent, of God, and of his miraculous ways and works amongst men, and of our religion and works, to be performed to him; after the story of our Saviour Christ, suffering to the lowest bent of weakness in the flesh, and presently triumphing to the highest pitch of glory in the spirit, which drew up his body also, till we in both be united to him in the revelation of his kingdom, I do not know of anything more worthy to take up the whole passion of pity on the one side, and joy on the other, than to consider first the foul and sudden corruption, and then, after many a tedious age, the long deferred, but much more wonderful and happy reformation of the church in these latter days. Sad it is to think how that doctrine of the gospel, planted by teachers divinely inspired, and by them winnowed and sifted from the chaff of overdated ceremonies, and refined to such a spiritual height and temper of purity, and knowledge of the Creator, that the body, with all the circumstances of time and place, were purified

by the affections of the regenerate soul, and nothing left impure but sin; faith needing not the
weak and fallible office of the senses, to be either
the ushers or interpreters of heavenly mysteries,
save where our Lord himself in his sacraments
ordained; that such a doctrine should, through
the grossness and blindness of her professors, and
the fraud of deceivable traditions, drag so down-
wards, as to backslide one way into the Jewish
beggary of old cast rudiments, and stumble forward another way into the new-vomited pagan-
ism of sensual idolatry, attributing purity or
impurity to things indifferent, that they might
bring the inward acts of the spirit to the outward
and customary eye-service of the body, as if they
could make God earthly and fleshly, because they
could not make themselves heavenly and spiritual;
they began to draw down all the divine intercourse
betwixt God and the soul, yea, the very shape of
God himself, into an exterior and bodily form,
urgently pretending a necessity and obligement of
joining the body in a formal reverence and worship circumscribed; they hallowed it, they fumed
it, they sprinkled it, they bedecked it, not in
robes of pure innocency, but of pure linen, with
other deformed and fantastic dresses, in palls and
mitres, gold, and gewgaws fetched from Aaron's old
wardrobe, or the Flamens' vestry : then was the
priest set to con his motions and his postures, his
liturgies and his lurries, till the soul by this means
of overbodying herself, given up justly to fleshly

delights, bated her wing apace downward: and finding the ease she had from her visible and sensuous
colleague, the body, in performance of religious
duties, her pinions now broken and flagging, shifted
off from herself the labour of high soaring any more,
forgot her heavenly flight, and left the dull and
droiling carcase to plod on in the old road and
drudging trade of outward conformity.   And here
out of question from her perverse conceiting of God
and holy things she had fallen to believe no God
at all, had not custom and the worm of conscience
nipped her incredulity : hence to all the duties of
evangelical grace, instead of the adoptive and
cheerful boldness which our new alliance with
God requires, came servile and thrall-like fear : for in
very deed the superstitious man by his good will
is an atheist ; but being scared from thence by the
pangs and gripes of a boiling conscience, all in a
pudder shuffles up to himself such a God and such
a worship as is most agreeable to remedy his fear ;
which fear of his, as also is his hope, fixed only upon
the flesh, renders likewise the whole faculty of his
apprehension carnal ; and all the inward acts of
worship, issuing from the native strength of the soul,
run out lavishly to the upper skin, and there harden
into a crust of formality.   Hence men came to
scan the scriptures by the letter, and in the covenant of our redemption magnified the external signs
more than the quickening power of the Spirit ;
and yet, looking on them through their own guiltiness with a servile fear, and finding as little com-

3

fort, or rather terror from them again, they knew not how to hide their slavish approach to God's behests, by them not understood, nor worthily received, but by cloaking their servile crouching to all religious presentments, sometimes lawful, sometimes idolatrous, under the name of humility, and terming the piebald frippery and ostentation of ceremonies, decency.

Then was baptism changed into a kind of exorcism, and water, sanctified by Christ's institute, thought little enough to wash off the original spot, without the scratch or cross impression of a priest's forefinger : and that feast of free grace and adoption to which Christ invited his disciples to sit as brethren, and co-heirs of the happy covenant, which at that table was to be sealed to them, even that feast of love and heavenly-admitted fellowship, the seal of filial grace, became the subject of horror, and glouting adoration, pageanted about like a dreadful idol ; which sometimes deceives well-meaning men, and beguiles them of their reward, by their voluntary humility ; which indeed is fleshly pride, preferring a foolish sacrifice, and the rudiments of the world, as St. Paul to the Colossians explaineth, before a savoury obedience to Christ's example. Such was Peter's unseasonable humility, as then his knowledge was small, when Christ came to wash his feet ; who at an impertinent time would needs strain courtesy with his master, and falling troublesomely upon the lowly, all-wise, and unexaminable intention of Christ, in

what he went with resolution to do, so provoked
by his interruption the meek Lord, that he threatened
to exclude him from his heavenly portion, unless he
could be content to be less arrogant and stiffnecked
in his humility.

But to dwell no longer in characterizing the de-
pravities of the church, and how they sprung, and
how they took increase ; when I recall to mind at
last, after so many dark ages wherein the huge
overshadowing train of error had almost swept all
the stars out of the firmament of the church, how
the bright and blissful Reformation (by divine
power) struck through the black and settled night
of ignorance and antichristian tyranny, methinks a
sovereign and reviving joy must needs rush into
the bosom of him that reads or hears, and the
sweet odour of the returning gospel imbathe his
soul with the fragrancy of heaven.   Then was
the sacred Bible sought out of the dusty corners
where profane falsehood and neglect had thrown
it, the schools opened, divine and human learning
raked out of the embers of forgotten tongues,
the princes and cities trooping apace to the new-
erected banner of salvation, the martyrs, with the
unresistible might of weakness, shaking the powers
of darkness, and scorning the fiery rage of the old
red dragon.

The pleasing pursuit of these thoughts hath
ofttimes led me into a serious question and debate-
ment with myself, how it should come to pass that
England (having had this grace and honour from

God, to be the first that should set up a standard
for the recovery of lost truth, and blow the first
evangelic trumpet to the nations, holding up, as
from a hill, the new lamp of saving light to all
Christendom) should now be last and most unsettled
in the enjoyment of that peace whereof she taught
the way to others; although indeed our Wicklef's
preaching, at which all the succeeding reformers
more effectually lighted their tapers, was to his
countrymen but a short blaze, soon damped and
stifled by the pope and prelates for six or seven
kings' reigns ; yet methinks the precedency which
God gave this island, to be first restorer of buried
truth, should have been followed with more happy
success, and sooner attained perfection ; in which
as yet we are amongst the last : for, albeit in purity
of doctrine we agree with our brethren, yet in
discipline, which is the execution and applying of
doctrine home, and laying the salve to the very
orifice of the wound, yea, tenting and searching to
the core, without which pulpit preaching is but
shooting at rovers—in this we are no better than a
schism from all the Reformation, and a sore scandal
to them : for while we hold ordination to belong
only to bishops, as our prelates do, we must of
necessity hold also their ministers to be no
ministers, and shortly after their church to be
no church : not to speak of those senseless ceremonies which we only retain as a dangerous
earnest of sliding back to Rome, and serving
merely either as a mist to cover nakedness where

true grace is extinguished or as an interlude to set out the pomp of prelatism. Certainly it would be worth the while therefore and the pains to inquire more particularly what and how many the chief causes have been, that have still hindered our uniform consent to the rest of the churches abroad, at this time especially when the kingdom is in a good propensity thereto, and all men in prayers, in hopes, or in disputes, either for or against it.

*   *   *   *   *   *   *
*   *   *   *   *   *

O, SIR, I do now feel myself inwrapt on the sudden into those mazes and labyrinths of dreadful and hideous thoughts, that which way to get out, or which way to end, I know not, unless I turn mine eyes, and with your help lift up my hands to that eternal and propitious throne, where nothing is readier than grace and refuge to the distresses of mortal suppliants: and it were a shame to leave these serious thoughts less piously than the heathen were wont to conclude their graver discourses.

Thou, therefore, that sittest in light and glory unapproachable, Parent of angels and men! next, thee I implore, omnipotent King, Redeemer of that lost remnant whose nature thou didst assume, ineffable and everlasting Love! and thou, the third subsistence of divine infinitude, illumining Spirit, the joy and solace of created things! one tri-personal Godhead! look upon this thy poor and almost spent and expiring church, leave her not thus a prey to these importunate wolves that wait and think long till they devour thy tender flock, these wild boars that have broke into thy vineyard and left the print of their polluting hoofs on the souls of thy servants. O let them not bring about their damned designs, that stand now at the entrance of the bottomless pit, expecting the watch-word to open and let out those dreadful locusts and scorpions, to reinvolve us in that pitchy cloud of infernal darkness, where we shall never more see the sun of thy truth again, never hope for the cheerful dawn, never more hear the bird of morning sing. Be moved with pity at the afflicted state of this our shaken monarchy, that now lies labouring under her throes and struggling against the grudges of more dreaded calamities.

O thou that after the impetuous rage of five bloody inundations, and the succeeding sword of intestine war, soaking the land in her own gore, didst pity the sad and ceaseless revolution of our swift and thick-coming sorrows; when we were quite breathless, of thy free grace didst motion peace, and terms of covenant with us; and having first well nigh freed us from antichristian thraldom didst build up this Britannic empire to a glorious and enviable height, with all her daughter-islands about her; stay us in this felicity, let not the obstinacy of our half-obedience and will-worship bring forth that viper of sedition that for these fourscore years hath been breeding to eat through the entrails of our peace, but let her cast her abortive spawn without the danger of this travail-ing and throbbing kingdom: that we may still remember in our solemn thanksgivings how for us the northern ocean even to the frozen Thule was scattered with the proud shipwrecks of the Spanish armada, and the very maw of hell ransacked and made to give up her concealed destruction, ere she could vent it in that horrible and damned blast.

O how much more glorious will those former deliverances appear when we shall know them not only to have saved us from greatest miseries past but to have reserved us for greatest happiness to come ! Hitherto thou hast but freed us, and that not fully, from the unjust and tyrannous claim of thy foes ; now unite us entirely and appropriate us to thyself, tie us everlastingly in willing homage to the prerogative of thy eternal throne.

And now we know, O thou our most certain hope and defence, that thine enemies have been consulting all the sorceries of the great Whore, and have joined their plots with that sad intelligencing tyrant that mischiefs the world with his mines of Ophir, and lies thirsting to revenge his naval ruins that have larded our seas : but let them all take counsel together, and let it come to nought ; let them decree, and do thou cancel it ; let them gather themselves, and be scattered ; let them embattle themselves, and be broken ; let them embattle, and be broken, for thou art with us.

Then, amidst the hymns and hallelujahs of saints, some one may perhaps be heard offering at high strains in new and lofty measure to sing and celebrate thy divine mercies and marvellous judgments in this land throughout all ages ; where-

by this great and warlike nation, instructed and
inured to the fervent and continual practice of truth
and righteousness, and casting far from her the rags
of her whole vices, may press on hard to that high
and happy emulation to be found the soberest,
wisest, and most Christian people at that day,
when thou, the eternal and shortly expected King,
shalt open the clouds to judge the several kingdoms
of the world, and distributing national honours and
rewards to religious and just commonwealths,
shalt put an end to all earthly tyrannies, proclaiming thy universal and mild monarchy through
heaven and earth ; where they undoubtedly, that
by their labours, counsels, and prayers, have been
earnest for the common good of religion and their
country, shall receive above the inferior orders of
the blessed the regal addition of principalities,
legions, and thrones into their glorious titles, and
in supereminence of beatific vision, progressing the
dateless and irrevoluble circle of eternity, shall
clasp inseparable hands with joy and bliss in
overmeasure for ever.

But they contrary that by the impairing and
diminution of the true faith, the distresses and
servitude of their country, aspire to high dignity,
rule, and promotion here, after a shameful end in
this life, (which God grant them,) shall be thrown
down eternally into the darkest and deepest gulf of
hell, where, under the despiteful control, the
trample and spurn of all the other damned, that in
the anguish of their torture, shall have no other

ease than to exercise a raving and bestial tyranny over them as their slaves and negroes, they shall remain in that plight for ever, the basest, the lower-most, the most dejected, most underfoot and down-trodden vassals of perdition.

REASON OF CHURCH GOVERNMENT

URGED AGAINST PRELATY.
IN TWO BOOKS. 1641.

The following extracts are from the beginning
and end of the Second Book

HOW happy were it for this frail and as it may
be truly called mortal life of man, since all
earthly things which have the name of good and
convenient in our daily use are withal so cumber-
some and full of trouble, if knowledge yet, which
is the best and lightsomest possession of the mind,
were, as the common saying is, no burden; and
that what it wanted of being a load to any part of
the body, it did not with a heavy advantage overlay
upon the spirit! For not to speak of that knowledge that rests in the contemplation of natural
causes and dimensions, which must needs be a
lower wisdom, as the object is low, certain it is,
that he who hath obtained in more than the scantiest
measure to know anything distinctly of God, and
of his true worship, and what is infallibly good
and happy in the state of man's life, what in itself
evil and miserable, though vulgarly not so esteemed; he that hath obtained to know this, the
only high valuable wisdom indeed, remembering

also that God, even to a strictness, requires the improvement of these his entrusted gifts, cannot but sustain a sorer burden of mind, and more pressing, than any supportable toil or weight which the body can labour under, how and in what manner he shall dispose and employ those sums of knowledge and illumination which God hath sent him into this world to trade with. And that which aggravates the burden more, is, that, having received amongst his allotted parcels certain precious truths of such an orient lusture as no diamond can equal, which nevertheless he has in charge to put off at any cheap rate, yea, for nothing to them that will ; the great merchants of this world, fearing that this course would soon discover and disgrace the false glitter of their deceitful wares, wherewith they abuse the people, like poor Indians with beads and glasses, practise by all means how they may suppress the vending of such rarities, and at such a cheapness as would undo them and turn their trash upon their hands. Therefore by gratifying the corrupt desires of men in fleshly doctrines they stir them up to persecute with hatred and contempt all those that seek to bear themselves uprightly in this their spiritual factory : which they foreseeing, though they cannot but testify of truth, and the excellency of that heavenly traffic which they bring, against what opposition or danger soever, yet needs must it sit heavily upon their spirits, that being, in God's prime intention and their own, selected heralds of peace

and dispensers of treasure inestimable, without
price, to them that have no peace, they find in the
discharge of their commission, that they are made
the greatest variance and offence, a very sword and
fire both in house and city over the whole earth.
This is that which the sad prophet Jeremiah
laments : 'Wo is me, my mother, that thou hast
'born me a man of strife and contention!' And
although divine inspiration must certainly have been
sweet to those ancient prophets, yet the irksomeness
of that truth which they brought was so unpleasant
unto them that everywhere they call it a burden.
Yea, that mysterious book of revelation, which the
great evangelist was bid to eat, as it had been
some eye-brightening electuary of knowledge and
foresight, though it were sweet in his mouth,
and in the learning, it was bitter in his belly,
bitter in the denouncing. Nor was this hid from
the wise poet Sophocles, who in that place of his
tragedy where Tiresias is called to resolve king
Œdipus in a matter which he knew would be grievous, brings him in bemoaning his lot, that he knew
more than other men. For surely to every good
peaceable man, it must in nature needs be a hateful
thing to be the displeaser and molester of thousands ;
much better would it like him doubtless to be the
messenger of gladness and contentment, which is
his chief intended business to all mankind, but
that they resist and oppose their own true happiness. But when God commands to take the trumpet, and blow a dolorous or a jarring blast, it lies

not in man's will what he shall say, or what he shall conceal. If he shall think to be silent as Jeremiah did, because of the reproach and derision he met with daily, 'And all his familiar friends 'watched for his halting,' to be revenged on him for speaking the truth, he would be forced to confess as he confessed: 'His word was in my heart 'as a burning fire shut up in my bones; I was weary 'with forbearing, and could not stay.' Which might teach these times not suddenly to condemn all things that are sharply spoken or vehemently written as proceeding out of stomach, virulence, and ill-nature; but to consider rather, that if the prelates have leave to say the worst that can be said, or do the worst that can be done, while they strive to keep to themselves, to their great pleasure and commodity, those things which they ought to render up, no man can be justly offended with him that shall endeavour to impart and bestow, without any gain to himself, those sharp but saving words which would be a terror and a torment in him to keep back. For me, I have determined to lay up as the best treasure and solace of a good old age, if God vouchsafe it me, the honest liberty of free speech from my youth, where I shall think it available in so dear a concernment as the church's good. For if I be, either by disposition or what other cause, too inquisitive, or suspicious of myself and mine own doings, who can help it? But this I foresee, that, should the church be brought under heavy oppres-

sion, and God have given me ability the while to
reason against that man that should be the author of
so foul a deed; or should she, by blessing from
above on the industry and courage of faithful men,
change this her distracted estate into better days,
without the least furtherance or contribution of
those few talents which God at that present had
lent me; I foresee what stories I should hear within
myself, all my life after, of discourage and reproach.
' Timorous and ungrateful, the church of God is now
' again at the foot of her insulting enemies, and thou
' bewailest. What matters it for thee or thy be-
' wailing? When time was, thou couldst not find
' a syllable of all that thou hast read or studied to
' utter in her behalf. Yet ease and leisure was given
' thee for thy retired thoughts, out of the sweat of
' other men. Thou hast the diligence, the parts,
' the language of a man, if a vain subject were to be
' adorned or beautified; but when the cause of God
' and his church was to be pleaded, for which pur-
' pose that tongue was given thee which thou hast,
' God listened if he could hear thy voice among his
' zealous servants, but thou wert dumb as a beast;
' from henceforward be that which thine own brutish
' silence hath made thee.' Or else I should have
heard on the other ear: ' Slothful, and ever to be set
' light by, the church hath now overcome her late
' distresses after unwearied labours of many her true
' servants that stood up in her defence; thou also
' wouldst take upon thee to share amongst them of
' their joy; but wherefore thou? Where canst thou

4

' shew any word or deed of thine which might have
' hastened her peace? Whatever thou dost now talk,
' or write, or look, is the alms of other men's active
' prudence and zeal. Dare not now to say or do any-
' thing better than thy former sloth and infancy; or if
' thou darest, thou dost impudently to make a thrifty
' purchase of boldness to thyself out of the painful
' merits of other men ; what before was thy sin is
' now thy duty, to be abject and worthless.' These,
and such-like lessons as these, I know would have
been my matins duly and my even-song.   But now
by this little diligence, mark what a privilege I
have gained with good men and saints, to claim my
right of lamenting the tribulations of the church, if
she should suffer, when others, that have ventured
nothing for her sake, have not the honour to be
admitted mourners.   But if she lift up her drooping
head and prosper, among those that have something more than wished her welfare, I have my
charter and freehold of rejoicing to me and my
heirs.   Concerning therefore this wayward subject
against prelaty, the touching whereof is so distaste-
ful and disquietous to a number of men, as by what
hath been said I may deserve of charitable readers
to be credited, that neither envy nor gall hath
entered me upon this controversy, but the enforcement of conscience only, and a preventive fear lest
the omitting of this duty should be against me,
when I would store up to myself the good provision
of peaceful hours : so, lest it should be still imputed
to me, as I have found it hath been, that some self-

pleasing humour of vain-glory hath incited me to
contest with men of high estimation, now while
green years are upon my head ; from this needless
surmisal I shall hope to dissuade the intelligent
and equal auditor, if I can but say successfully that
which in this exigent behoves me ; although I
would be heard only, if it might be, by the elegant
and learned reader, to whom principally for a while
I shall beg leave I may address myself.   To him
it will be no new thing, though I tell him that if I
hunted after praise by the ostentation of wit and
learning, I should not write thus out of mine own
season when I have neither yet completed to my
mind the full circle of my private studies, although
I complain not of any insufficiency to the matter in
hand ; or were I ready to my wishes, it were a
folly to commit anything elaborately composed to
the careless and interrupted listening of these
tumultuous times.   Next, if I were wise only to
my own ends, I would certainly take such a subject
as of itself might catch applause, whereas this hath
all the disadvantages on the contrary, and such a
subject as the publishing whereof might be delayed
at pleasure, and time enough to pencil it over with
all the curious touches of art, even to the perfection
of a faultless picture ; whenas in this argument the
not deferring is of great moment to the good speed-
ing, that if solidity have leisure to do her office, art
cannot have much.   Lastly, I should not choose
this manner of writing, wherein knowing myself
inferior to myself, led by the genial power of

nature to another task, I have the use, as I may account, but of my left hand. And though I shall be foolish in saying more to this purpose, yet, since it will be such a folly as wisest men go about to commit, having only confessed and so committed, I may trust with more reason, because with more folly, to have courteous pardon. For although a poet, soaring in the high reason of his fancies, with his garland and singing robes about him, might without apology speak more of himself than I mean to do ; yet for me sitting here below in the cool element of prose, a mortal thing among many readers of no empyreal conceit, to venture and divulge unusual things of myself, I shall petition to the gentler sort, it may not be envy to me. I must say therefore that after I had for my first years, by the ceaseless diligence and care of my father, (whom God recompense) been exercised to the tongues, and some sciences, as my age would suffer, by sundry masters and teachers, both at home and at the schools, it was found that whether aught was imposed me by them that had the overlooking, or betaken to of mine own choice in English or other tongue, prosing or versing, but chiefly by this latter, the style, by certain vital signs it had, was likely to live. But much latelier in the private academies of Italy, whither I was favoured to resort, perceiving that some trifles which I had in memory, composed at under twenty or thereabout, (for the manner is, that every one must give some proof of his wit and reading there,) met with acceptance above what was looked for ; and other things, which I had shifted in scarcity of books and conveniences to patch up amongst them, were received with written encomiums, which the Italian is not forward to bestow on men of this side the Alps ; I began thus far to assent both to them and divers of my friends here at home, and not less to an inward prompting which now grew daily upon me, that by labour and intent study, (which I take to be my portion in this life,) joined with the strong propensity of nature, I might perhaps leave something so written to aftertimes as they should not willingly let it die. These thoughts at once possessed me, and these other ; that if I were certain to write as men buy leases, for three lives and downward, there ought no regard be sooner had than to God's glory, by the honour and instruction of my country. For which cause, and not only for that I knew it would be hard to arrive at the second rank among the Latins, I applied myself to that resolution which Ariosto followed against the persuasions of Bembo, to fix all the industry and art I could unite to the adorning of my native tongue ; not to make verbal curiosities the end, (that were a toilsome vanity,) but to be an interpreter and relater of the best and sagest things among mine own citizens throughout this island in the mother dialect. That what the greatest and choicest wits of Athens, Rome, or modern Italy, and those Hebrews of old did for their country, I, in my proportion, with this over and above of being a

Christian, might do for mine; not caring to be once named abroad, though perhaps I could attain to that, but content with these British islands as my world; whose fortune hath hitherto been, that if the Athenians, as some say, made their small deeds great and renowned by their eloquent writers, England hath had her noble achievements made small by the unskilful handling of monks and mechanics.

Time serves not now, and perhaps I might seem too profuse to give any certain account of what the mind at home, in the spacious circuits of her musing, hath liberty to propose to herself, though of highest hope and hardest attempting; whether that epic form whereof the two poems of Homer, and those other two of Virgil and Tasso, are a diffuse, and the book of Job a brief model: or whether the rules of Aristotle herein are strictly to be kept, or nature to be followed, which in them that know art and use judgment is no transgression but an enriching of art: and lastly, what king or knight, before the conquest, might be chosen in whom to lay the pattern of a Christian hero. And as Tasso gave to a prince of Italy his choice whether he would command him to write of Godfrey's expedition against the Infidels, or Belisarius against the Goths, or Charlemain against the Lombards; if to the instinct of nature and the emboldening of art aught may be trusted, and that there be nothing adverse in our climate, or the fate of this age, it haply would be no rashness, from an equal diligence

and inclination, to present the like offer in our
own ancient stories; or whether those dramatic
constitutions, wherein Sophocles and Euripides
reign, shall be found more doctrinal and exemplary
to a nation.   The scripture also affords us a divine
pastoral drama in the Song of Solomon, consisting
of two persons and a double chorus, as Origen
rightly judges.   And the Apocalypse of St. John
is the majestic image of a high and stately tragedy,
shutting up and intermingling her solemn scenes
and acts with a sevenfold chorus of hallelujahs and
harping symphonies : and this my opinion the
grave authority of Pareus, commenting that book,
is sufficient to confirm.   Or if occasion shall lead,
to imitate those magnific odes and hymns, wherein
Pindarus and Callimachus are in most things
worthy, some others in their frame judicious, in
their matter most and end faulty.   But those frequent songs throughout the law and prophets
beyond all these, not in their divine argument
alone, but in the very critical art of composition,
may be easily made appear over all the kinds of
lyric poesy to be incomparable.   These abilities,
wheresoever they be found, are the inspired gift of
God, rarely bestowed, but yet to some (though
most abuse) in every nation ; and are of power,
beside the office of a pulpit, to imbreed and cherish
in a great people the seeds of virtue and public
civility, to allay the perturbations of the mind, and
set the affections in right tune ; to celebrate in
glorious and lofty hymns the throne and equipage

of God's almightiness, and what he works and what he suffers to be wrought with high providence in his church ; to sing victorious agonies of martys and saints, the deeds and triumphs of just and pious nations, doing valiantly through faith against the enemies of Christ ; to deplore the general relapses of kingdoms and states from justice and God's true worship.   Lastly, whatsoever in religion is holy and sublime, in virtue amiable or grave, whatso-ever hath passion or admiration in all the changes of that which is called fortune from without, or the wily subtleties and refluxes of man's thoughts from within ; all these things with a solid and treatable smoothness to paint out and describe.   Teaching over the whole book of sanctity and virtue, through all the instances of example, with such delight to those especially of soft and delicious temper, who will not so much as look upon truth herself, unless they see her elegantly dressed ; that whereas the paths of honesty and good life appear now rugged and difficult, though they be indeed easy and pleasant, they will then appear to all men both easy and pleasant, though they were rugged and difficult indeed.   And what a benefit this would be to our youth and gentry, may be soon guessed by what we know of the corruption and bane which they suck in daily from the writings and interludes of libidinous and ignorant poetasters, who having scarce ever heard of that which is the main con-sistence of a true poem, the choice of such persons as they ought to introduce, and what is moral and

decent to each one; do for the most part lay up
vicious principles in sweet pills to be swallowed
down, and make the taste of virtuous documents
harsh and sour. But because the spirit of man
cannot demean itself lively in this body without
some recreating intermission of labour and serious
things, it were happy for the commonwealth if our
magistrates, as in those famous governments of
old, would take into their care not only the de-
ciding of our contentious law-cases and brawls
but the managing of our public sports and festival
pastimes; that they might be, not such as were
authorized a while since, the provocations of
drunkenness and lust, but such as may inure and
harden our bodies by martial exercises to all warlike skill and performance; and may civilize,
adorn, and make discreet our minds by the learned
and affable meeting of frequent academies, and the
procurement of wise and artful recitations, sweet-
ened with eloquent and graceful enticements to the
love and practice of justice, temperance, and
fortitude, instructing and bettering the nation at
all opportunities, that the call of wisdom and
virtue may be heard everywhere, as Solomon
saith : 'She crieth without, she uttereth her voice
' in the streets, in the top of high places, in the chief
' concourse, and in the openings of the gates.'
Whether this may not be, not only in pulpits, but
after another persuasive method, at set and solemn
paneguries, in theatres, porches, or what other
place or way may win most upon the people to

receive at once both recreation and instruction, let
them in authority consult.   The thing which I had
to say, and those intentions which have lived
within me ever since I could conceive myself anything worth to my country, I return to crave excuse
that urgent reason hath plucked from me, by an
abortive and foredated discovery.   And the accomplishment of them lies not but in a power
above man's to promise ; but that none hath by
more studious ways endeavoured, and with more
unwearied spirit that none shall, that I dare almost
aver of myself, as far as life and free leisure will
extend ; and that the land had once enfranchised
herself from this impertinent yoke of prelaty,
under whose inquisitorious and tyrannical duncery
no free and splendid wit can flourish.   Neither do
I think it a shame to covenant with any knowing
reader, that for some few years yet I may go on
trust with him toward the payment of what I am
now indebted, as being a work not to be raised
from the heat of youth, or the vapours of wine,
like that which flows at waste from the pen of some
vulgar amourist, or the trencher fury of a rhyming
parasite ; nor to be obtained by the invocation of
dame Memory and her siren daughters, but by
devout prayer to that eternal Spirit who can enrich
with all utterance and knowledge, and sends out
his seraphim with the hallowed fire of his altar
to touch and purify the lips of whom he pleases :
to this must be added industrious and select
reading, steady observation, insight into all seemly

and generous arts and affairs; till which in some
measure be compassed, at mine own peril and cost,
I refuse not to sustain this expectation from as
many as are not loth to hazard so much credulity
upon the best pledges that I can give them.
Although it nothing content me to have disclosed
thus much beforehand, but that I trust hereby to
make it manifest with what small willingness I
endure to interrupt the pursuit of no less hopes than
these, and leave a calm and pleasing solitariness,
fed with cheerful and confident thoughts, to em-
bark in a troubled sea of noises and hoarse disputes,
put from beholding the bright countenance of truth
in the quiet and still air of delightful studies, to
come into the dim reflection of hollow antiquities
sold by the seeming bulk, and there be fain to club
quotations with men whose learning and belief lies
in marginal stuffings, who, when they have, like
good sumpters, laid ye down their horse-loads of
citations and fathers at your door, with a rhapsody
of who and who were bishops here or there, ye
may take off their packsaddles, their day's work
is done, and episcopacy, as they think, stoutly
vindicated. Let any gentle apprehension, that can
distinguish learned pains from unlearned drudgery
imagine what pleasure or profoundness can be in
this, or what honour to deal against such adversaries. But were it the meanest under-service, if
God by his secretary conscience enjoin it, it were
sad for me if I should draw back; for me especially, now when all men offer their aid to help,

ease, and lighten the difficult labours of the church, to whose service, by the intentions of my parents and friends, I was destined of a child, and in mine own resolutions : till coming to some maturity of years, and perceiving what tyranny had invaded the church, that he who would take orders must subscribe slave, and take an oath withal, which, unless he took with a conscience that would retch, he must either straight perjure, or split his faith ; I thought it better to prefer a blameless silence before the sacred office of speaking bought and begun with servitude and forswearing. Howsoever, thus church-outed by the prelates, hence may appear the right I have to meddle in these matters, as before the necessity and constraint appeared.

* * * * * * *

* * * * * * *

The Mischief that Prelaty does in the State.

I ADD one thing more to those great ones that are so fond of prelaty: this is certain, that the gospel being the hidden might of Christ, as hath been heard, that ever a victorious power joined with it, like him in the Revelation that went forth on the white horse with his bow and his crown, conquering and to conquer. If we let the angel of the gospel ride on his own way, he does his proper business, conquering the high thoughts and the proud reasonings of the flesh, and brings them under to give obedience to Christ with the salvation of many souls. But if ye turn him out of his road, and in a manner force him to express his irresistible power by a doctrine of carnal might, as prelaty is, he will use that fleshly strength which ye put into his hands to subdue your spirits by a servile and blind superstition; and that again shall hold such dominion over your captive minds, as returning with an insatiate greediness and force upon your worldly wealth and power, wherewith to deck and magnify herself and her false worships, he shall spoil and havoc your estates, disturb your ease, diminish your honour, enthral your liberty under the swelling mood of a proud clergy, who will not serve or feed your souls with spiritual food; look not for it, they have not wherewithal, or if they had, it is not in their purpose. But when they have glutted their ungrateful bodies, at least if it be possible that those open sepulchres should ever be glutted, and when they have stuffed their idolish temples with the wasteful pillage of your estates, will they yet have any compassion upon you, and that poor pittance which they have left you; will they be but so good to you as that ravisher was to his sister, when he had used her at his pleasure; will they but only hate ye, and so turn ye loose? No, they will not, lords and commons, they will not favour ye so much. What will they do then, in the name of God and saints, what will these manhaters yet with more despite and mischief do? I will tell ye, or at least remember ye: (for most of ye know it already:) that they may want nothing to make them true merchants of Babylon, as they have done to your souls, they will sell your bodies, your wives, your children, your liberties, your parliaments, all these things; and if there be ought else dearer than these, they will sell at an outcry in their pulpits to the arbitrary and illegal dispose of any one that may hereafter be called a king, whose mind shall serve him to listen to their bargain. And by their corrupt and servile doctrines boring our ears to an everlasting slavery, as they have done hitherto,

so will they yet do their best to repeal and erase
every line and clause of both our great charters.
Nor is this only what they will do, but what they
·hold as the main reason and mystery of their advancement that they must do ; be the prince never
so just and equal to his subjects, yet such are their
malicious and depraved eyes, that they so look on
him and so understand him as if he required no
other gratitude or piece of service from them than
this. And indeed they stand so opportunely for the
disturbing or the destroying of a state, being a knot
of creatures whose dignities, means, and preferments have no foundation in the gospel, as they
themselves acknowledge, but only in the prince's
favour, and to continue so long to them, as by
pleasing him they shall deserve : whence it must
needs be they should bend all their intentions and
services to no other ends but to his, that if it
should happen that a tyrant (God turn such a
scourge from us to our enemies) should come to
grasp the sceptre, here were his spearmen and his
lances, here were his firelocks ready, he should
need no other pretorian band nor pensionary than
these, if they could once with their perfidious
preachments awe the people. For although the
prelates in time of popery were sometimes friendly
enough to Magna Charta, it was because they
stood upon their own bottom, without their main
dependance on the royal nod : but now being well
acquainted that the protestant religion, if she will
reform herself rightly by the scriptures, must

undress them of all their gilded vanities and reduce them as they were at first to the lowly and
equal order of presbyters, they know it concerns
them nearly to study the times more than the text,
and to lift up their eyes to the hills of the court,
from whence only comes their help ; but if their
pride grow weary of this crouching and observance,
as ere long it would, and that yet their minds
climb still to a higher ascent of worldly honour,
this only refuge can remain to them, that they
must of necessity contrive to bring themselves and
us back again to the pope's supremacy ; and this
we see they had by fair degrees of late been doing.
These be the two fair supporters between which
the strength of prelaty is borne up, either of in-
ducing tyranny, or of reducing popery. Hence
also we may judge that prelaty is mere falsehood.
For the property of truth is, where she is publicly
taught to unyoke and set free the minds and
spirits of a nation first from the thraldom of sin
and superstition, after which all honest and legal
freedom of civil life cannot be long absent ; but prelaty, whom the tyrant custom begot, a natural tyrant in religion, and in state the agent and minister
of tyranny, seems to have had this fatal gift in her
nativity, like another Midas, that whatsoever she
should touch or come near either in ecclesial or
political government, it should turn, not to gold,
though she for her part could wish it, but to the
dross and scum of slavery, breeding and settling
both in the bodies and the souls of all such as do

not in time, with the sovereign treacle of sound doctrine, provide to fortify their hearts against her hierarchy. The service of God, who is truth, her liturgy confesses to be perfect freedom ; but her works and her opinions declare that the service of prelaty is perfect slavery, and by consequence perfect falsehood. Which makes me wonder much that many of the gentry, studious men as I hear, should engage themselves to write and speak publicly in her defence ; but that I believe their honest and ingenuous natures coming to the universities to store themselves with good and solid learning, and there unfortunately fed with nothing else but the scragged and thorny lectures of monkish and miserable sophistry, were sent home again with such a scholastic bur in their throats as hath stopped and hindered all true and generous philosophy from entering, cracked their voices for ever with metaphysical gargarisms, and hath made them admire a sort of formal outside men prelatically addicted, whose unchastened and unwrought minds were never yet initiated or subdued under the true lore of religion or moral virtue, which two are the best and greatest points of learning ; but either slightly trained up in a kind of hypocritical and hackney course of literature to get their living by, and dazzle the ignorant, or else fondly over-studied in useless controversies, except those which they use with all the specious and delusive subtlety they are able, to defend their prelatical Sparta ; having a gospel and church government set before their

5

eyes, as a fair field. wherein they might exercise
the greatest virtues and the greatest deeds of
Christian authority in mean fortunes and little
furniture of this world ;, (which even the sage
heathen writers and those old Fabritii and Curii
well knew to be a manner of working than which
nothing could liken a mortal man more to God,
who delights most to work from within himself,
and not by the heavy luggage of corporeal instruments ;) they understand it not, and think no such
matter, but admire and dote upon worldly riches
and honours, with an easy and intemperate life, to
the bane of Christianity : yea, they and their semi-
naries shame not to profess, to petition, and never
leave pealing our ears, that unless we fat them
like boars, and cram them as they list with wealth,
with deaneries and pluralities, with baronies and
stately preferments, all learning and religion will
go underfoot. Which is such a shameless, such a
bestial plea, and of that odious impudence in
churchmen, who should be to us a pattern of temperance and frugal mediocrity, who should teach
us to contemn this world and the gaudy things
thereof, according to the promise which they themselves require from us in baptism, that should the
scripture stand by and be mute, there is not that
sect of philosophers among the heathen so dissolute, no not Epicurus, nor Aristippus with all
his Cyrenaic rout, but would shut his school-doors
against such greasy sophisters ; not any college of
mountebanks but would think scorn to discover in

themselves with such a brazen forehead the outrageous desire of filthy lucre.   Which the prelates
make so little conscience of, that they are ready to
fight and, if it lay in their power, to massacre all
good Christians under the names of horrible schismatics, for only finding fault with their temporal
dignities, their unconscionable wealth and revenues,
their cruel authority over their brethren that labour
in the word while they snore in their luxurious
excess : openly proclaiming themselves now in the
sight of all men to be those which for a while
they sought to cover under sheep's clothing, ravenous and savage wolves, threatening inroads and
bloody incursions upon the flock of Christ, which
they took upon them to feed, but now claim to
devour as their prey.   More like that huge dragon
of Egypt, breathing out waste and desolation to
the land, unless he were daily fattened with virgin's blood.   Him our old patron St. George by
his matchless valour slew, as the prelate of the
garter that reads his collect can tell.   And if our
princes and knights will imitate the fame of that
old champion, as by their order of knighthood
solemnly taken they vow, far be it that they should
uphold and side with this English dragon ; but
rather to do as indeed their oaths bind them, they
should make it their knightly adventure to pursue
and vanquish this mighty sail-winged monster,
that menaces to swallow up the land, unless her
bottomless gorge may be satisfied with the blood
of the king's daughter, the church ; and may, as

she was wont, fill her dark and infamous den with
the bones of the saints.   Nor will any one have
reason to think this as too incredible or too
tragical to be spoken of prelaty, if he consider well
from what a mass of slime and mud, the slothful
the covetous, and ambitious hopes of church-pro-
motions and fat bishoprics, she is bred up and
muzzled in, like a great Python, from her youth,
to prove the general poison both of doctrine and
good discipline in the land.   For certainly such
hopes and such principles of earth as these wherein
she welters from a young one, are the immediate
generation both of a slavish and tyrannous life to
follow, and a pestiferous contagion to the whole
kingdom, till like that fen-born serpent she be
shot to death with the darts of the sun, the pure
and powerful beams of God's word.   And this
may serve to describe to us in part what prelaty
hath been, and what, if she stand, she is like to be
toward the whole body of people in England.
Now that it may appear how she is not such a
kind of evil as hath any good or use in it, which
many evils have, but a distilled quintessence, a
pure elixir of mischief, pestilent alike to all, I shall
shew briefly, ere I conclude, that the prelates, as
they are to the subjects a calamity, so are they the
greatest underminers and betrayers of the monarch,
to whom they seem to be most favourable.   I cannot better liken the state and person of a king than
to that mighty Nazarite Samson ; who being disciplined from his birth in the precepts and the

practice of temperance and sobriety, without the
strong drink of injurious and excessive desires,
grows up to a noble strength and perfection with
those his illustrious and sunny locks, the laws,
waving and curling about his godlike shoulders.
And while he keeps them about him undiminished
and unshorn, he may with the jawbone of an ass,
that is, with the word of his meanest officer, suppress and put to confusion thousands of those that
rise against his just power. But laying down his
head among the strumpet flatteries of prelates,
while he sleeps and thinks no harm, they wickedly
shaving off all those bright and weighty tresses of
his law, and just prerogatives, which were his
ornament and strength, deliver him over to indi-
rect and violent counsels, which, as those Philistines, put out the fair and far-sighted eyes of his
natural discerning, and make him grind in the
prisonhouse of their sinister ends and practices
upon him : till he, knowing this prelatical rasor to
have bereft him of his wonted might, nourish again
his puissant hair, the golden beams of law and
right ; and they sternly shook, thunder with ruin
upon the heads of those his evil counsellors, but
not without great affliction to himself. This is the
sum of their loyal service to kings ; yet these are
the men that still cry, The king, the king, the
Lord's anointed ! We grant it ; and wonder how
they came to light upon anything so true ; and
wonder more, if kings be the Lord's anointed, how
they dare thus oil over and besmear so holy an

unction with the corrupt and putrid ointment of
their base flatteries; which while they smooth the
skin, strike inward and envenom the lifeblood.
What fidelity kings can expect from prelates, both
examples past and our present experience of their
doings at this day, whereon is grounded all that
hath been said, may suffice to inform us. And if
they be such clippers of regal power and shavers
of the laws, how they stand affected to the law-
giving parliament, yourselves, worthy peers and
commons, can best testify; the current of whose
glorious and immortal actions hath been only op-
posed by the obscure and pernicious designs of the
prelates, until their insolence broke out to such a
bold affront as hath justly immured their haughty
looks within strong walls. Nor have they done
anything of late with more diligence than to hinder or break the happy assembling of parliaments,
however needful to repair the shattered and dis-
jointed frame of the commonwealth; or if they
cannot do this, to cross, to disenable, and traduce
all parliamentary proceedings. And this, if nothing else, plainly accuses them to be no lawful
members of the house, if they thus perpetually
mutiny against their own body. And though they
pretend, like Solomon's harlot, that they have
right thereto, by the same judgment that Solomon
gave it cannot belong to them, whenas it is not
only their assent but their endeavour continually
to divide parliaments in twain; and not only by
dividing but by all other means to abolish and

destroy the free use of them to all posterity. For
the which, and for all their former misdeeds,
whereof this book and many volumes more cannot
contain the moiety, I shall move ye, lords, in the
behalf I dare say of many thousand good Christians, to let your justice and speedy sentence pass
against this great malefactor, prelaty. And yet in
the midst of rigour I would beseech ye to think of
mercy; and such a mercy, (I fear I shall overshoot
with a desire to save this falling prelaty,) such a
mercy (if I may venture to say it) as may exceed
that which for only ten righteous persons would
have saved Sodom. Not that I dare advise ye to
contend with God, whether he or you shall be
more merciful, but in your wise esteems to balance
the offences of those peccant cities with these enor-
mous riots of ungodly misrule that prelaty hath
wrought both in the church of Christ and in the
state of this kingdom. And if ye think ye may
with a pious presumption strive to go beyond God
in mercy, I shall not be one now that would dissuade ye. Though God for less than ten just persons
would not spare Sodom, yet if you can find, after
due search, but only one good thing in prelaty,
either to religion or civil government, to king or
parliament, to prince or people, to law, liberty,
wealth, or learning, spare her, let her live, let her
spread- among ye, till with her shadow all your
dignities and honours and all the glory of the land
be darkened and obscured. But on the contrary,
if she be found to be malignant, hostile, destructive

to all these, as nothing can be surer, then let your severe and impartial doom imitate the divine vengeance ; rain down your punishing force upon this godless and oppressing government, and bring such a dead sea of subversion upon her, that she may never in this land rise more to afflict the holy reformed church, and the elect people of God.

ANIMADVERSIONS UPON THE REMONSTRANT'S DEFENCE AGAINST SMECTYMNUUS

1641.

Smectymnuus was a signature composed of the initials of the names of five writers of a pamphlet against episcopacy, controverted by Bishop Hall and supported by Milton.

The following extracts are from the fourth and thirteenth of thirteen sections.

ANIMADVERSIONS UPON THE RE-MONSTRANT'S DEFENCE AGAINST SMECTYMNUUS.

IF you require a further answer, it will not mis-become a Christian to be either more mag-nanimous or more devout than Scipio was; who, instead of other answer to the frivolous accusations of Petilius the tribune, "This day, Romans, (saith he,) I fought with Hannibal prosperously; let us all go and thank the gods that gave us so great a victory:" in like manner will we now say, not caring otherwise to answer this unprotestantlike objection : In this age, Britons, God hath reformed his church after many hundred years of popish corruption; in this age he hath freed us from the intolerable yoke of prelates and papal discipline; in this age he hath renewed our protestation against all those yet remaining dregs of superstition. Let us all go, every true protested Briton, throughout the three kingdoms, and render thanks to God the Father of light and Fountain of heavenly grace, and to his Son Christ our Lord, leaving this Re-monstrant and his adherents to their own designs; and let us recount even here without delay the

patience and. long-suffering that God hath used
toward our blindness and hardness time after time.
For he being equally near to his whole creation of
mankind, and of free power to turn his beneficent
and fatherly regard to what region or kingdom he
pleases, hath yet ever had this island under the
special indulgent eye of his providence ; and pitying
us the first of all other nations, after he had decreed
to purify and renew his church that lay wallowing
in idolatrous pollutions, sent first to us a healing
messenger to touch softly our sores and carry a
gentle hand over our wounds : he knocked once
and twice, and came again opening our drowsy
eyelids leisurely by that glimmering light which
Wicklef and his followers dispersed ; and still
taking off by degrees the inveterate scales from our
nigh perished sight, purged also our deaf ears, and
prepared them to attend his second warning trumpet
in our grandsires' days.   How else could they have
been able to have received the sudden assault of
his reforming Spirit, warring against human principles, and carnal sense, the pride of flesh, that
still cried up antiquity, custom, canons, councils,
and laws, and cried down the truth for novelty,
schism, profaneness, and sacrilege? whenas we that
have lived so long in abundant light, besides the
sunny reflection of all the neighbouring churches,
have yet our hearts rivetted with those old opinions,
and so obstructed and benumbed with the same
fleshly reasonings, which in our forefathers soon
melted and gave way, against the morning beam of

reformation. If God had left undone this whole
work, so contrary to flesh and blood, till these
times, how should we have yielded to his heavenly
call, had we been taken, as they were, in the
starkness of our ignorance ; that yet, after all these
spiritual preparatives and purgations, have our
earthly apprehensions so clammed and furred with
the old leaven? O if we freeze at noon after their
early thaw, let us fear lest the sun for ever hide
himself and turn his orient steps from our ingrateful horizon, justly condemned to be eternally be-
nighted. Which dreadful judgment, O thou the
ever-begotten Light and perfect Image of the
Father ! intercede may never come upon us, as we
trust thou hast ; for thou hast opened our difficult
and sad times, and given us an unexpected breathing after our long oppressions: thou hast done
justice upon those that tyrannized over us, while
some men wavered and admired a vain shadow of
wisdom in a tongue nothing slow to utter guile,
though thou hast taught us to admire only that
which is good, and to count that only praiseworthy
which is grounded upon thy divine precepts. Thou
hast discovered the plots, and frustrated the hopes,
of all the wicked in the land, and put to shame the
persecutors of thy church : thou hast made our
false prophets to be found a lie in the sight of all
the people, and chased them with sudden confusion
and amazement before the redoubled brightness of
thy descending cloud, that now covers thy taber-
nacle. Who is there that cannot trace thee now in

thy beamy walk through the midst of thy sanctuary, amid those golden candlesticks, which have long suffered a dimness among us through the violence of those that had seized them, and were more taken with the mention of their gold than of their starry light, teaching the doctrine of Balaam, to cast a stumbling-block before thy servants, commanding them to eat things sacrificed to idols, and forcing them to fornification? Come therefore, O thou that hast the seven stars in thy right hand, appoint thy chosen priests according to their orders and courses of old, to minister before thee, and duly to press and pour out the consecrated oil into thy holy and ever-burning lamps. Thou hast sent out the spirit of prayer upon thy servants over all the land to this effect, and stirred up their vows as the sound of many waters about thy throne. Every one can say that now certainly thou hast visited this land, and hast not forgotten the utmost corners of the earth, in a time when men had thought that thou wast gone up from us to the furthest end of the heavens, and hadst left to do marvellously among the sons of these last ages. O perfect and accomplish thy glorious acts! for men may leave their works unfinished, but thou art a God, thy nature is perfection: shouldst thou bring us thus far onward from Egypt to destroy us in this wilderness, though we deserve, yet thy great name would suffer in the rejoicing of thine enemies, and the deluded hope of all thy servants. When thou hast settled peace in the church, and righteous judgment

in the kingdom, then shall all thy saints address
their voices of joy and triumph to thee, standing on
the shore of that Red Sea into which our enemies
had almost driven us. And he that now for haste
snatches up a plain ungarnished present as a thank-
offering to thee, which could not be deferred in
regard of thy so many late deliverances wrought
for us one upon another, may then perhaps take up
a harp, and sing thee an elaborate song to genera-
tions. In that day it shall no more be said as in
scorn, this or that was never held so till this present
age, when men have better learnt that the times
and seasons pass along under thy feet to go and
come at thy bidding : and as thou didst dignify our
fathers' days with many revelations above all the
foregoing ages since thou tookest the flesh; so
thou canst vouchsafe to us (though unworthy) as
large a portion of thy Spirit as thou pleasest : for
who shall prejudice thy all-governing will? seeing
the power of thy grace is not passed away with the
primitive times, as fond and faithless men imagine,
but thy kingdom is now at hand, and thou standing
at the door. Come forth out of thy royal chambers,
O Prince of all the kings of the earth ! put on the
visible robes of thy imperial majesty, take up that
unlimited sceptre which thy Almighty Father hath
bequeathed thee; for now the voice of thy bride
calls thee, and all creatures sigh to be renewed.

* * * * * * *

This is the root of all our mischief, that which
they allege for the encouragement of their studies

should be cut away forewith as the very bait of pride and ambition, the very garbage that draws together all the fowls of prey and ravine in the land to come and gorge upon the church. How can it be but ever unhappy to the church of England, while she shall think to entice men to the pure service of God by the same means that were used to tempt our Saviour to the service of the devil, by laying before him honour and preferment? Fit professors indeed are they like to be to teach others that godliness with content is great gain, whenas their godliness of teaching had not been but for worldly gain. The heathen philosophers thought that virtue was for its own sake inestimable, and the greatest gain of a teacher to make a soul virtuous; so Xenophon writes to Socrates, who never bargained with any for teaching them; he feared not lest those who had received so high a benefit from him would not of their own free will return him all possible thanks. Was moral virtue so lovely and so alluring, and heathen men so enamoured of her as to teach and study her with greatest neglect and contempt of worldly profit and advancement? And is Christian piety so homely and so unpleasant, and Christian men so cloyed with her, as that none will study and teach her but for lucre and preferment? O stale grown piety! O gospel rated as cheap as thy Master, at thirty pence, and not worth the study unless thou canst buy those that will sell thee! O race of Capernaïtans, senseless of divine

doctrine, and capable only of loaves and belly-
cheer ! But they will grant, perhaps, piety may
thrive, but learning will decay : I would fain ask
these men at whose hands they seek inferior things,
as wealth, honour, their dainty fare, their lofty
houses ? No doubt but they will soon answer,
that all these things **they seek at** God's hands.
Do they think then that all these meaner and
superfluous things come from God, and the divine
gift of learning from the den of Plutus, or the cave
of Mammon ? Certainly never any clear spirit
nursed up from brighter influences, with **a** soul
enlarged to the dimensions of spacious **art** and high
knowledge, ever entered there but with scorn, and
thought it ever foul disdain to make pelf **or** ambition the reward of his studies ; it being the
greatest honour, the greatest fruit and proficiency
of learned studies to despise these things. Not
liberal science but illiberal must that needs be
that mounts in contemplation merely for money.
And what would it avail us to have **a** hireling
clergy, though never so learned? **For** such can
have neither true wisdom nor grace ; and then in
vain do men trust in learning where these be
wanting. **If** in **less** noble and almost mechanic
arts, according to the definitions of those authors,
he is not esteemed to deserve the name of a complete architect, an excellent painter, or the like,
that bears not a generous mind above the peasantly
regard of wages and hire ; much more must we
think him **a** most imperfect and incomplete divine

6

who is so far from being a contemner of filthy lucre that his whole divinity is moulded and bred up in the beggarly and brutish hopes of a fat prebendary, deanery, or bishopric ; which poor and low-pitched desires, if they do but mix with those other heavenly intentions that draw a man to this study, it is justly expected that they should bring forth a baseborn issue of divinity, like that of those imperfect and putrid creatures that receive a crawling life from two most unlike procreants, the sun and mud. And in matters of religion, there is not anything more intolerable than a learned fool, or a learned hypocrite : the one is ever cooped up at his empty speculations, a sot, an idiot for any use that mankind can make of him, or else sowing the world with nice and idle questions, and with much toil and difficulty wading to his auditors up to the eyebrows in deep shallows that wet not the instep : a plain unlearned man that lives well by that light which he has, is better and wiser and edifies others more towards a godly and happy life than he. The other is still using his sophisticated arts, and bending all his studies how to make his insatiate avarice and ambition seem pious and orthodoxal, by painting his lewd and deceitful principles with a smooth and glossy varnish in a doctrinal way, to bring about his wickedest purposes. Instead of the great harm therefore that these men fear upon the dissolving of prelates, what an ease and happiness will it be to us when tempting rewards are taken away, that the cunningest and most dangerous mercenaries

will cease of themselves to frequent the fold, whom
otherwise scarce all the prayers of the faithful could
have kept back from devouring the flock! But a
true pastor of Christ's sending hath this especial
mark, that for greatest labours and greatest merits
in the church he requires either nothing, if he
could so subsist, or a very common and reasonable
supply of human necessaries. We cannot therefore do better than to leave this care of ours to
God: he can easily send labourers into his harvest,
that shall not cry, Give, give, but be contented
with a moderate and beseeming allowance; nor
will he suffer true learning to be wanting where
true grace and our obedience to him abounds:
for if he give us to know him aright, and to
practise this our knowledge in right-established
discipline, how much more will he replenish us
with all abilities in tongues and arts that may
conduce to his glory and our good! He can stir
up rich fathers to bestow exquisite education upon
their children, and so dedicate them to the service
of the gospel; he can make the sons of nobles his
ministers, and princes to be his Nazarites; for
certainly there is no employment more honourable,
more worthy to take up a great spirit, more re-
quiring a generous and free nurture, than to be the
messenger and herald of heavenly truth from God
to man, and by the faithful work of holy doctrine
to procreate a number of faithful men, making a
kind of creation like to God's, by infusing his spirit
and likeness into them, to their salvation, as God
did into him; arising to what climate soever he

turn him, like that Sun of Righteousness that
sent him, with healing in his wings, and new light
to break in upon the chill and gloomy hearts of
his hearers, raising out of darksome barrenness a
delicious and fragrant spring of saving knowledge
and good works. Can a man thus employed find
himself discontented or dishonoured for want of
admittance to have a pragmatical voice at sessions
and jail deliveries? or because he may not as a
judge sit out the wrangling noise of litigious courts
to shrive the purses of unconfessing and unmor-
tified sinners, and not their souls, or be discouraged
though men call him not lord, whenas the due
performance of his office would gain him, even
from lords and princes, the voluntary title of
father? Would he tug for a barony to sit and vote
in parliament, knowing that no man can take from
him the gift of wisdom and sound doctrine, which
leaves him free, though not to be a member, yet a
teacher and persuader of the parliament? And in
all wise apprehensions the persuasive power in man
to win others to goodness by instruction is greater
and more divine than the compulsive power to
restrain men from being evil by terror of the law;
and therefore Christ left Moses to be the lawgiver,
but himself came down among us to be a teacher,
with which office his heavenly wisdom was so well
pleased as that he was angry with those that
would have put a piece of temporal judicature into
his hands, disclaiming that he had any commission
from above for such matters.

* * * * * * *

AN APOLOGY FOR SMECTYMNUUS

1642.

The following extracts are both taken from near the middle
of the Apology.

WITH me it fares now as with him whose outward garment hath been injured and ill-bedighted; for having no other shift, what help but to turn the inside outward, especially if the lining be of the same, or, as it is sometimes, much better? So if my name and outward demeanour be not evident enough to defend me, I must make trial if the discovery of my inmost thoughts can: wherein of two purposes, both honest and both sincere, the one perhaps I shall not miss; although I fail to gain belief with others, of being such as my perpetual thoughts shall here disclose me, I may yet not fail of success in persuading some to be such really themselves, as they cannot believe me to be more than what I feign.

I had my time, readers, as others have, who have good learning bestowed upon them, to be sent to those places where, the opinion was, it might be soonest attained; and as the manner is, was not unstudied in those authors which are most commended. Whereof some were grave orators and historians, whose matter methought I loved indeed, but as my age then was, so I understood them; others were the smooth elegaic poets, whereof the schools are not scarce, whom both for the pleasing sound of their numerous writing, which in imitation I found most easy and most agreeable to nature's part in me, and for their matter, which what it is there be few who know not, I was so allured to read that no recreation came to me better welcome. For that it was then those years with me which are excused, though they be least severe, I may be saved the labour to remember ye. Whence having observed them to account it the chief glory of their wit, in that they were ablest to judge, to praise, and by that could esteem themselves worthiest to love those high perfections which under one or other name they took to celebrate; I thought with myself by every instinct and presage of nature, which is not wont to be false, that what emboldened them to this task might with such diligence as they used embolden me; and that what judgment, wit, or elegance was my share, would herein best appear, and best value itself, by how much more wisely and with more love of virtue I should choose (let rude ears be absent) the object of not unlike praises. For albeit these thoughts to some will seem virtuous and commendable, to others only pardonable, to a third sort perhaps idle; yet the mentioning of them now will end in serious.

Nor blame it, readers, in those years to propose to themselves such a reward as the noblest dispositions above other things in this life have some-

times preferred : whereof not to be sensible when
good and fair in one person meet, argues both a
gross and shallow judgment and withal an un-
gentle and swainish breast. For by the firm
settling of these persuasions I became, to my best
memory, so much a proficient that if I found
those authors anywhere speaking unworthy things
of themselves, or unchaste of those names which
before they had extolled, this effect it wrought
with me ; from that time forward their art I still
applauded, but the men I deplored ; and above
them all preferred the two famous renowners of
Beatrice and Laura, who never write but honour
of them to whom they devote their verse, display-
ing sublime and pure thoughts, without transgression. And long it was not after, when I was
confirmed in this opinion, that he who would not
be frustrate of his hope to write well hereafter in
laudable things ought himself to be a true poem ;
that is, a composition and pattern of the best and
honourablest things ; not presuming to sing high
praises of heroic men, or famous cities, unless he
have in himself the experience and the practice of
all that which is praiseworthy. These reasonings,
together with a certain niceness of nature, an
honest haughtiness, and self-esteem either of what
I was, or what I might be, (which let envy call
pride,) and lastly that modesty, whereof, though
not in the title-page, yet here I may be excused to
make some beseeming profession ; all these uniting
the supply of their natural aid together, kept me

still above those low descents of mind beneath which he must deject and plunge himself that can agree to saleable and unlawful prostitutions.

Next, (for hear me out now, readers,) that I may tell ye whither my younger feet wandered; I betook me among those lofty fables and romances which recount in solemn cantos the deeds of knighthood founded by our victorious kings and from hence had in renown over all Christendom. There I read it in the oath of every knight, that he should defend to the expense of his best blood, or of his life, if it so befell him, the honour and chastity of virgin or matron; from whence even then I learned what a noble virtue chastity sure must be, to the defence of which so many worthies, by such a dear adventure of themselves, had sworn. And if I found in the story afterward any of them, by word or deed, breaking that oath, I judged it the same fault of the poet as that which is attributed to Homer, to have written indecent things of the gods. Only this my mind gave me, that every free and gentle spirit, without that oath, ought to be born a knight, nor needed to expect the gilt spur or the laying of a sword upon his shoulder to stir him up both by his counsel and his arms to secure and protect the weakness of any attempted chastity. So that even these books, which to many others have been the fuel of wantonness and loose living, I cannot think how, unless by divine indulgence, proved to me so many incitements, as you have heard, to the love and steadfast observation of that virtue which abhors the society of bordelloes.

Thus, from the laureat fraternity of poets, riper years and the ceaseless round of study and reading led me to the shady spaces of philosophy; but chiefly to the divine volumes of Plato, and his equal Xenophon: where, if I should tell ye what I learnt of chastity and love, I mean that which is truly so, whose charming cup is only virtue, which she bears in her hand to those who are worthy; (the rest are cheated with a thick intoxicating potion, which a certain sorceress, the abuser of love's name, carries about;) and how the first and chiefest office of love begins and ends in the soul, producing those happy twins of her divine generation, knowledge and virtue; with such abstracted sublimities as these, it might be worth your listening, readers, as I may one day hope to have ye in a still time, when there shall be no chiding; not in these noises, the adversary, as ye know, barking at the door, or searching for me at the bordelloes, where it may be he has lost himself, and raps up without pity the sage and rheumatic old prelatesse, with all her young Corinthian laity, to inquire for such a one.

Last of all, not in time, but as perfection is last, that care was ever had of me, with my earliest capacity, not to be negligently trained in the precepts of the Christian religion: this that I have hitherto related hath been to shew that though Christianity had been but slightly taught me, yet a certain reservedness of natural disposition, and moral discipline, learnt out of the noblest philosophy, was enough to keep me in disdain of far less incontinences than this of the bordello. But having had the doctrine of holy scripture unfolding those chaste and high mysteries with timeliest care infused, that 'the body is for the Lord, and 'the Lord for the body;' thus also I argued to myself, that if unchastity in a woman, whom St. Paul terms the glory of man, be such a scandal and dishonour, then certainly in a man, who is both the image and glory of God, it must, though commonly not so thought, be much more deflouring and dishonourable; in that he sins both against his own body, which is the perfecter sex, and his own glory, which is in the woman; and, that which is worst, against the image and glory of God, which is in himself. Nor did I slumber over that place expressing such high rewards of ever accompanying the Lamb, with those celestial songs to others inapprehensible, but not to those who were not defiled with women, which doubtless means fornication; for marriage must not be called a defilement.

Thus large I have purposely been, that if I have been justly taxed with this crime, it may come upon me, after all this my confession, with a tenfold shame: but if I have hitherto deserved no such opprobrious word, or suspicion, I may hereby engage myself now openly to the faithful observation of what I have professed.

* * * * * * *

But to the end that nothing may be omitted which may farther satisfy any conscionable man, who notwithstanding what I could explain before the Animadversions, remains yet unsatisfied concerning that way of writing which I there defended, but this confuter, whom it pinches, utterly disapproves; I shall assay once again, and perhaps with more success. If therefore the question were in oratory, whether a vehement vein throwing out indignation or scorn upon an object that merits it, were among the aptest *ideas* of speech to be allowed, it were my work, and that an easy one, to make it clear both by the rules of best rhetoricians and the famousest examples of the Greek and Roman orations. But since the religion of it is disputed, and not the art, I shall make use only of such reasons and authorities as religion cannot except against. It will be harder to gainsay than for me to evince that in the teaching of men diversely tempered different ways are to be tried. The Baptist, we know, was a strict man, remarkable for austerity and set order of life. Our Saviour, who had all gifts in him, was Lord to express his indoctrinating power in what sort him best seemed; sometimes by a mild and familiar converse; sometimes with plain and impartial home-speaking, regardless of those whom the auditors might think he should have had in more respect; otherwhile, with bitter and ireful rebukes, if not teaching, yet leaving excuseless those his wilful impugners.

What was all in him, was divided among many others the teachers of his church ; some to be severe and ever of a sad gravity, that they may win such, and check sometimes those who be of nature over-confident and jocund ; others were sent more cheerful, free, and still as it were at large, in the midst of an untrespassing honesty ; that they who are so tempered may have by whom they might be drawn to salvation, and they who are too scrupulous, and dejected of spirit, might be often strengthened with wise consolations and revivings : no man being forced wholly to dissolve that groundwork of nature which God created in him, the sanguine to empty out all his sociable liveliness, the choleric to expel quite the unsinning predominance of his anger ; but that each radical humour and passion, wrought upon and corrected as it ought, might be made the proper mould and foundation of every man's peculiar gifts and virtues. Some also were indued with a staid moderation and soundness of argument, to teach and convince the rational and sober-minded ; yet not therefore that to be thought the only expedient course of teaching, for in times of opposition, when either against new heresies arising or old corruptions to be reformed this cool unpassionate mildness of positive wisdom is not enough to damp and astonish the proud resistance of carnal and false doctors, then (that I may have leave to soar awhile as the poets use) Zeal, whose substance is ethereal, arming in complete diamond, ascends his fiery chariot,

drawn with two blazing meteors, figured like
beasts, but of a higher breed than any the zodiac
yields, resembling two of those four which Ezekiel
and St. John saw ; the one visaged like a lion, to
express power, high authority, and indignation ;
the other of countenance like a man, to cast derision
and scorn upon perverse and fraudulent seducers :
with these the invincible warrior, Zeal, shaking
loosely the slack reins, drives over the heads of
scarlet prelates and such as are insolent to maintain traditions, bruising their stiff necks under his
flaming wheels.

*   *   *   *   *   *   *

THE DOCTRINE AND DISCIPLINE OF DIVORCE

RESTORED, TO THE GOOD OF BOTH
SEXES, FROM THE BONDAGE OF
CANON LAW AND OTHER MIS-
TAKES TO THE TRUE MEANING OF
SCRIPTURE IN THE LAW AND
GOSPEL COMPARED.

WHEREIN ALSO ARE SET DOWN
THE BAD CONSEQUENCES OF ABO-
LISHING, OR CONDEMNING AS SIN,
THAT WHICH THE LAW OF GOD
ALLOWS AND CHRIST ABOLISHED
NOT: IN TWO BOOKS: TO THE
PARLIAMENT OF ENGLAND WITH
THE ASSEMBLY. 1644.

7

Matth. xiii. 52. "Every scribe instructed in the kingdom of heaven is like the master of a house, which bringeth out of his treasury things new and old."

Prov. xviii. 13. "He that answereth a matter before he heareth it, it is folly and shame unto him."

The following extract consists of the sixth chapter of Book I, entitled "The Fourth Reason of this Law, that God regards Love and Peace in the Family more than a compulsive Performance of Marriage, which is more broke by a grievous Continuance than by a needful Divorce."

FOURTHLY, Marriage is a covenant, the very being whereof consists not in a forced cohabitation and counterfeit performance of duties, but in unfeigned love and peace : and of matrimonial love, no doubt but that was chiefly meant, which by the ancient sages was thus parabled ; that Love, if he be not twin born, yet hath a brother wondrous like him, called Anteros ; whom while he seeks all about, his chance is to meet with many false and feigning desires that wander singly up and down in his likeness : by them in their borrowed garb, Love, though not wholly blind, as poets wrong him, yet having but one eye, as being born an archer aiming, and that eye not the quickest in this dark region here below, which is not Love's proper sphere, partly out of the simplicity and credulity which is native to him, often deceived, embraces and consorts him with these obvious and suborned striplings, as if they were his mother's own sons ; for so he thinks them, while they subtilly keep themselves most on his blind side. But after a while, as his manner is, when soaring up into the high tower of his Apogæum, above the shadow of the earth, he darts out the direct rays of his then most piercing eyesight upon the impostures and trim disguises that were used with him, and discerns that this is not his genuine brother, as he imagined ; he has no longer the power to hold fellowship with such a personated mate : for straight his arrows lose their golden heads and shed their purple feathers, his silken braids untwine and slip their knots, and that original and fiery virtue given him by fate all on a sudden goes out, and leaves him undeified and despoiled of all his force ; till finding Anteros at last, he kindles and repairs the almost-faded ammunition of his deity by the reflection of a coequal and homogeneal fire. Thus mine author sung it to me : and by the leave of those who would be counted the only grave ones, this is no mere amatorious novel ; (though to be wise and skilful in these matters, men heretofore of greatest name in virtue have esteemed it one of the highest arcs that human contemplation circling upwards can make from the globy sea whereon she stands ;) but this is a deep and serious verity, shewing us that love in marriage cannot live nor subsist unless it be mutual ; and where love cannot be, there can be left of wedlock nothing but the empty husk of an outside matrimony, as undelightful and unpleasing to God as any other kind of hypocrisy. So far is his command from tying men to the observance of duties which there is no help for, but they must be dissembled. If Solomon's advice be not over-frolic, 'Live joyfully,' saith he, 'with the wife whom 'thou lovest, all thy days, for that is thy portion :' how then, where we find it impossible to rejoice or to love, can we obey this precept? How miserably do we defraud ourselves of that comfortable por- tion which God gives us, by striving vainly to glue an error together which God and nature will not join, adding but more vexation and violence to that blissful society by our importunate superstition, that will not hearken to St. Paul, 1 Cor. vii., who, speaking of marriage and divorce, determines plain enough in general that God therein 'hath called 'us to peace, and not to bondage!' Yea, God himself commands in his law more than once, and by his prophet Malachi, as Calvin and the best translations read, that 'he who hates, let him 'divorce,' that is, he who cannot love. Hence it is that the rabbins, and Maimonides, famous among the rest, in a book of his set forth by Buxtorfius, tells us, that 'divorce was permitted by Moses to 'preserve peace in marriage, and quiet in the 'family.' Surely the Jews had their saving peace about them as well as we ; yet care was taken that this wholesome provision for household peace should also be allowed them : and must this be denied to Christians? O perverseness! that the law should be made more provident of peace- making than the gospel ! that the gospel should be put to beg a most necessary help of mercy from the

law, but must not have it ! and that to grind in the
mill of an undelighted and servile copulation must
be the only forced work of a Christian marriage,
ofttimes with such a yokefellow, from whom both
love and peace, both nature and religion mourn to
be separated. I cannot therefore be so diffident
as not securely to conclude, that he who can
receive nothing of the most important helps in
marriage, being thereby disenabled to return that
duty which is his with a clear and hearty countenance, and thus continues to grieve whom he
would not, and is no less grieved ; that man ought
even for love's sake and peace to move divorce
upon good and liberal conditions to the divorced.
And it is a less breach of wedlock to part with
wise and quiet consent betimes than still to foil
and profane that mystery of joy and union with a
polluting sadness and perpetual distemper : for it
is not the outward continuing of marriage that
keeps whole that covenant, but whatsoever does
most according to peace and love, whether in
marriage or in divorce, he it is that breaks marriage
least ; it being so often written, that ' Love only
' is the fulfilling of every commandment.'

*   *   *   *   *   *   *

ON EDUCATION

TO MASTER SAMUEL HARTLIB. 1644.

I AM long since persuaded, Master Hartlib, that to say or do aught worth memory and imitation, no purpose or respect should sooner move us than simply the love of God and of mankind. Nevertheless to write now the reforming of education, though it be one of the greatest and noblest designs that can be thought on, and for the want whereof this nation perishes, I had not yet at this time been induced, but by your earnest entreaties and serious conjurements, as having my mind for the present half diverted in the pursuance of some other assertions, the knowledge and the use of which cannot but be a great furtherance both to the enlargement of truth, and honest living with much more peace. Nor should the laws of any private friendship have prevailed with me to divide thus or transpose my former thoughts, but that I see those aims, those actions, which have won you with me the esteem of a person sent hither by some good providence from a far country to be the occasion and incitement of great good to this island.

And, as I hear, you have obtained the same repute with men of most approved wisdom, and some of the highest authority among us ; not to mention the learned correspondence which you hold in foreign parts, and the extraordinary pains and diligence which you have used in this matter, both here and beyond the seas; either by the definite will of God so ruling, or the peculiar sway of nature, which also is God's working. Neither can I think that, so reputed and so valued as you are, you would, to the forfeit of your own discerning ability, impose upon me an unfit and over-ponderous argument ; but that the satisfaction which you profess to have received from those incidental discourses which we have wandered into, hath pressed and almost constrained you into a persuasion, that what you require from me in this point I neither ought nor can in conscience defer beyond this time both of so much need at once and so much opportunity to try what God hath determined.

I will not resist, therefore, whatever it is, either of divine or human obligement, that you lay upon me ; but will forthwith set down in writing, as you request me, that voluntary idea which hath long in silence presented itself to me, of a better education, in extent and comprehension far more large, and yet of time far shorter, and of attainment far more certain, than hath been yet in practice. Brief I shall endeavour to be ; for that which I have to say, assuredly this nation hath extreme need should be done sooner than spoken. To tell you, therefore, what I have benefited herein

among old renowned authors, I shall spare ; and
to search what many modern Januas and Didactics,
more than ever I shall read, have projected, my
inclination leads me not. But if you can accept
of these few observations which have flowered off,
and are as it were the burnishing of many studious
and contemplative years, altogether spent in the
search of religious and civil knowledge, and such
as pleased you so well in the relating, I here give
you them to dispose of.

The end then of learning is to repair the ruins
of our first parents by regaining to know God
aright, and out of that knowledge to love him, to
imitate him, to be like him, as we may the nearest
by possessing our souls of true virtue, which being
united to the heavenly grace of faith makes up
the highest perfection. But because our understanding cannot in this body found itself but on
sensible things, nor arrive so clearly to the knowledge of God and things invisible as by orderly
conning over the visible and inferior creature, the
same method is necessarily to be followed in all
discreet teaching. And seeing every nation affords
not experience and tradition enough for all kinds
of learning, therefore we are chiefly taught the
languages of those people who have at any time
been most industrious after wisdom ; so that language is but the instrument conveying to us things
useful to be known. And though a linguist should
pride himself to have all the tongues that Babel
cleft the world into, yet if he have not studied the

solid things in them, as well as the words and lexicons, he were nothing so much to be esteemed a learned man as any yeoman or tradesman competently wise in his mother dialect only.

Hence appear the many mistakes which have made learning generally so unpleasing and so unsuccessful; first, we do amiss to spend seven or eight years merely in scraping together so much miserable Latin and Greek as might be learned otherwise easily and delightfully in one year. And that which casts our proficiency therein so much behind is our time lost partly in too oft idle vacancies given both to schools and universities; partly in a preposterous exaction, forcing the empty wits of children to compose themes, verses, and orations, which are the acts of ripest judgment and the final work of a head filled by long reading and observing with elegant maxims and copious invention. These are not matters to be wrung from poor striplings, like blood out of the nose, or the plucking of untimely fruit. Besides the ill habit which they get of wretched barbarizing against the Latin and Greek idiom with their untutored Anglicisms, odious to be read, yet not to be avoided without a well-continued and judicious conversing among pure authors digested, which they scarce taste. Whereas if after some preparatory grounds of speech by their certain forms got into memory, they were led to the praxis thereof in some chosen short book lessoned thoroughly to them, they might then forthwith proceed to learn the substance of good things, and arts in due order, which would bring the whole language quickly into their power. This I take to be the most rational and most profitable way of learning languages, and whereby we may best hope to give account to God of our youth spent herein.

And for the usual method of teaching arts, I deem it to be an old error of universities, not yet well recovered from the scholastic grossness of barbarous ages, that instead of beginning with arts most easy, (and those be such as are most obvious to the sense,) they present their young unmatriculated novices, at first coming, with the most intellective abstractions of logic and metaphysics; so that they having but newly left those grammatic flats and shallows, where they stuck unreasonably to learn a few words with lamentable construction, and now on the sudden transported under another climate, to be tossed and turmoiled with their unballasted wits in fathomless and unquiet deeps of controversy, do for the most part grow into hatred and contempt of learning, mocked and deluded all this while with ragged notions and babblements, while they expected worthy and delightful knowledge; till poverty or youthful years call them importunately their several ways, and hasten them, with the sway of friends, either to an ambitious and mercenary, or ignorantly zealous divinity: some allured to the trade of law, grounding their purposes not on the prudent and heavenly contemplation of justice and equity,

which was never taught them, but on the promising
and pleasing thoughts of litigious terms, fat con-
tentions, and flowing fees ; others betake them
to state affairs, with souls so unprincipled in virtue
and true generous breeding that flattery and court-
shifts and tyrannous aphorisms appear to them
the highest points of wisdom ; instilling their
barren hearts with a conscientious slavery ; if, as I
rather think, it be not feigned.   Others, lastly, of
a more delicious and airy spirit, retire themselves
(knowing no better) to the enjoyments of ease and
luxury, living out their days in feast and jollity ;
which indeed is the wisest and safest course of all
these, unless they were with more integrity under-
taken.   And these are the errors, and these are
the fruits of mis-spending our prime youth at the
schools and universities as we do, either in learning
mere words, or such things chiefly as were better
unlearned.

I shall detain you now no longer in the demonstration of what we should not do, but straight
conduct you to a hill-side, where I will point you
out the right path of a virtuous and noble education ; laborious indeed at the first ascent, but else
so smooth, so green, so full of goodly prospect and
melodious sounds on every side that the harp of
Orpheus was not more charming.   I doubt not but
ye shall have more ado to drive our dullest and
laziest youth, our stocks and stubs, from the infinite desire of such a happy nurture, than we have
now to hale and drag our choicest and hopefullest

wits to that asinine feast of sowthistles and brambles which is commonly set before them as all the food and entertainment of their tenderest and most docible age. I call therefore a complete and generous education, that which fits a man to perform justly, skilfully, and magnanimously all the offices, both private and public, of peace and war. And how all this may be done between twelve and one and twenty, less time than is now bestowed in pure trifling at grammar and sophistry, is to be thus ordered.

First, to find out a spacious house and ground about it fit for an academy, and big enough to lodge a hundred and fifty persons, whereof twenty or thereabout may be attendants, all under the government of one, who shall be thought of desert sufficient, and ability either to do all or wisely to direct and oversee it done. This place should be at once both school and university, not needing a remove to any other house of scholarship, except it be some peculiar college of law, or physic, where they mean to be practitioners; but as for those general studies which take up all our time from Lily to commencing, as they term it, master of art, it should be absolute. After this pattern, as many edifices may be converted to this use as shall be needful in every city throughout this land, which would tend much to the increase of learning and civility everywhere. This number, less or more, thus collected, to the convenience of a foot company, or interchangeably two troops of cavalry, should divide their day's work into three parts as it lies orderly; their studies, their exercise, and their diet.

For their studies: first, they should begin with the chief and necessary rules of some good grammar, either that now used or any better; and while this is doing, their speech is to be fashioned to a distinct and clear pronunciation, as near as may be to the Italian, especially in the vowels. For we Englishmen, being far northerly, do not open our mouths in the cold air wide enough to grace a southern tongue; but are observed by all other nations to speak exceeding close and inward, so that to smatter Latin with an English mouth is as ill a hearing as law French. Next, to make them expert in the usefullest points of grammar, and withal to season them and win them early to the love of virtue and true labour, ere any flattering seducement or vain principle seize them wandering, some easy and delightful book of education would be read to them, whereof the Greeks have store, as Cebes, Plutarch, and other Socratic discourses. But in Latin we have none of classic authority extant, except the two or three first books of Quinctilian, and some select pieces elsewhere.

But here the main skill and groundwork will be to temper them such lectures and explanations, upon every opportunity, as may lead and draw them in willing obedience, inflamed with the study of learning and the admiration of virtue, stirred up with high hopes of living to be brave men and

worthy patriots, dear to God, and famous to all
ages, that they may despise and scorn all their
childish and ill-taught qualities, to delight in manly
and liberal exercises, which he who hath the art
and proper eloquence to catch them with, what with
mild and effectual persuasions, and what with the
intimation of some fear, if need be, but chiefly by
his own example, might in a short space gain them
to an incredible diligence and courage, infusing into
their young breasts such an ingenuous and noble
ardour as would not fail to make many of them
renowned and matchless men. At the same time,
some other hour of the day, might be taught them
the rules of arithmetic ; and soon after the elements
of geometry, even playing, as the old manner was.
After evening repast, till bedtime, their thoughts
would be best taken up in the easy grounds of
religion, and the story of scripture.

The next step would be to the authors of agri-
culture, Cato, Varro, and Columella, for the matter
is most easy; and if the language be difficult, so
much the better, it is not a difficulty above their
years. And here will be an occasion of inciting
and enabling them hereafter to improve the tillage
of their country, to recover the bad soil, and to
remedy the waste that is made of good ; for this
was one of Hercules' praises. Ere half these authors
be read (which will soon be with plying hard and
daily) they cannot choose but be masters of any
ordinary prose. So that it will be then seasonable
for them to learn in any modern author the use of

the globes, and all the maps first with the old
names and then with the new; 'or they might be
then capable to read any compendious method of
natural philosophy.   And at the same time might
be entering into the Greek tongue, after the same
manner as was before prescribed in the Latin;
whereby the difficulties of grammar being soon
overcome, all the historical physiology of Aristotle
and Theophrastus are open before them, and, as I
may say, under contribution.   The like access will
be to Vitruvius, to Seneca's natural questions, to
Mela, Celsus, Pliny, or Solinus.   And having
thus passed the principles of arithmetic, geometry,
astronomy, and geography, with a general compact
of physics, they may descend in mathematics to the
instrumental science of trigonometry, and from
thence to fortification, architecture, enginery, or
navigation.   And in natural philosophy they may
proceed leisurely from the history of meteors,
minerals, plants, and living creatures, as far as
anatomy.

Then also in course might be read to them, out
of some not tedious writer, the institution of physic, that they may know the tempers, the humours,
the seasons, and how to manage a crudity; which
he who can wisely and timely do, is not only a
great physician to himself and to his friends, but also
may, at some time or other, save an army by this
frugal and expenseless means only; and not let the
healthy and stout bodies of young men rot away
under him for want of this discipline; which is a

great pity, and no less a shame to the commander.
To set forward all these proceedings in nature and
mathematics, what hinders but that they may pro-
cure, as oft as shall be needful, the helpful experience of hunters, fowlers, fishermen, shepherds,
gardeners, apothecaries? and in the other sciences,
architects, engineers, mariners, anatomists; who
doubtless would be ready, some for reward, and
some to favour such a hopeful seminary. And this
will give them such a real tincture of natural
knowledge as they shall never forget, but daily
augment with delight. Then also those poets which
are now counted most hard will be both facile and
pleasant, Orpheus, Hesiod, Theocritus, Aratus,
Nicander, Oppian, Dionysius; and in Latin,
Lucretius, Manilius, and the rural part of Virgil.

By this time, years and good general precepts
will have furnished them more distinctly with that
act of reason which in ethics is called *Proairesis*;
that they may with some judgment contemplate
upon moral good and evil. Then will be required
a special reinforcement of constant and sound indoctrinating, to set them right and firm, instructing
them more amply in the knowledge of virtue and
the hatred of vice; while their young and pliant
affections are led through all the moral works of
Plato, Xenophon, Cicero, Plutarch, Laertius, and
those Locrian remnants of Timaeus; but still to be
reduced in their nightward studies, wherewith they
close the day's work, under the determinate sentence of David or Solomon or the evangelists and

apostolic scriptures. Being perfect in the knowledge of personal duty they may then begin the study of economics. And either now, or before this, they may have easily learned, at any odd hour, the Italian tongue. And soon after, but with wariness and good antidote, it would be wholesome enough to let them taste some choice comedies, Greek, Latin, or Italian ; those tragedies also, that treat of household matters, as Trachiniæ, Alcestis, and the like.

The next removal must be to the study of politics ; to know the beginning, end, and reasons of political societies ; that they may not, in a dangerous fit of the commonwealth, be such poor, shaken, uncertain reeds, of such a tottering conscience, as many of our great counsellors have lately shewn themselves, but steadfast pillars of the state. After this, they are to dive into the grounds of law, and legal justice ; delivered first and with best warrant by Moses ; and as far as human prudence can be trusted, in those extolled remains of Grecian lawgivers, Lycurgus, Solon, Zaleucus, Charondas, and thence to all the Roman edicts and tables with their Justinian ; and so down to the Saxon and common laws of England, and the statutes.

Sundays also and every evening may be now understandingly spent in the highest matters of theology, and church history ancient and modern ; and ere this time the Hebrew tongue at a set hour might have been gained, that the Scriptures may be now read in their own original ; whereto it would be no impossibility to add the Chaldee and the Syrian dialect. When all these employments are well conquered, then will the choice histories, heroic poems, and Attic tragedies of stateliest and most regal argument, with all the famous political orations, offer themselves ; which if they were not only read, but some of them got by memory, and solemnly pronounced with right accent and grace, as might be taught, would endue them even with the spirit and vigour of Demosthenes or Cicero, Euripides or Sophocles.

And now, lastly, will be the time to read with them those organic arts which enable men to discourse and write perspicuously, elegantly, and according to the fittest style, of lofty, mean, or lowly. Logic, therefore, so much as is useful, is to be referred to this due place with all her well-couched heads and topics, until it be time to open her contracted palm into a graceful and ornate rhetoric, taught out of the rule of Plato, Aristotle, Phalereus, Cicero, Hermogenes, Longinus. To which poetry would be made subsequent, or indeed rather precedent, as being less subtile and fine, but more simple, sensuous, and passionate. I mean not here the prosody of a verse, which they could not but have hit on before among the rudiments of grammar ; but that sublime art which in Aristotle's Poetics, in Horace, and the Italian commentaries of Castelvetro, Tasso, Mazzoni, and others, teaches what the laws are of a true epic poem, what of a dramatic, what of a lyric, what decorum is, which is the grand masterpiece to observe. This would make them soon perceive what despicable creatures our common rhymers and play-writers be ; and shew them what religious, what glorious and magnificent use might be made of poetry, both in divine and human things.

From hence, and not till now, will be the right season of forming them to be able writers and composers in every excellent matter, when they shall be thus fraught with an universal insight into things. Or whether they be to speak in parliament or council, honour and attention would be waiting on their lips. There would then also appear in pulpits other visage, other gestures, and stuff otherwise wrought than what we now sit under, ofttimes to as great a trial of our patience as any other that they preach to us. These are the studies wherein our noble and our gentle youth ought to bestow their time, in a disciplinary way, from twelve to one and twenty : unless they rely more upon their ancestors dead than upon themselves living. In which methodical course it is so supposed they must proceed by the steady pace of learning onward, as at convenient times, for memory's sake, to retire back into the middle ward, and sometimes into the rear of what they have been taught, until they have confirmed and solidly united the whole body of their perfected knowledge, like the embattling of a Roman legion. Now will be worth the seeing, what exercises and recreations may best agree, and become these studies.

The course of study hitherto briefly described is, what I can guess by reading, likest to those ancient and famous schools of Pythagoras, Plato, Isocrates, Aristotle, and such others, out of which were bred such a number of renowned philosophers, orators, historians, poets, and princes all over Greece, Italy, and Asia, besides the flourishing studies of Cyrene and Alexandria. But herein it shall exceed them, and supply a defect as great as that which Plato noted in the commonwealth of Sparta ; whereas that city trained up their youth most for war, and these in their academies and Lycæum all for the gown, this institution of breeding which I here delineate shall be equally good both for peace and war. Therefore about an hour and a half ere they eat at noon should be allowed them for exercise, and due rest afterwards ; but the time for this may be enlarged at pleasure, according as their rising in the morning shall be early.

The exercise which I commend first is the exact use of their weapon, to guard, and to strike safely with edge or point ; this will keep them healthy, nimble, strong, and well in breath ; it is also the likeliest means to make them grow large and tall, and to inspire them with a gallant and fearless courage, which being tempered with seasonable lectures and precepts to them of true fortitude and patience, will turn into a native and heroic valour, and make them hate the cowardice of doing wrong. They must be also practised in all the locks and gripes of wrestling, wherein Englishmen were wont to excel, as need may often be in fight to tug, to grapple, and to close. And this perhaps will be enough, wherein to prove and heat their single strength.

The interim of unsweating themselves regularly, and convenient rest before meat, may, both with profit and delight, be taken up in recreating and composing their travailed spirits with the solemn and divine harmonies of music, heard or learned ; either while the skilful organist plies his grave and fancied descant in lofty fugues, or the whole symphony with artful and unimaginable touches adorn and grace the well-studied chords of some choice composer ; sometimes the lute or soft organ-stop waiting on elegant voices, either to religious, martial, or civil ditties ; which, if wise men and prophets be not extremely out, have a great power over dispositions and manners, to smooth and make them gentle from rustic harshness and distempered passions. The like also would not be inexpedient after meat, to assist and cherish nature in her first concoction, and send their minds back to study in good tune and satisfaction. Where having followed it close under vigilant eyes till about two hours before supper, they are, by a sudden alarum or watchword, to be called out to their military motions, under sky or covert, according to the season, as was the Roman wont ; first on foot, then, as their age permits, on horseback, to all the art of cavalry ; that having in sport, but with much exactness and daily muster, served out the rudiments of their soldiership, in all the skill of embattling, marching, encamping, fortifying, besieging, and battering, with all the helps of ancient and modern stratagems, tactics, and warlike maxims, they may as it were out of a long war come forth renowned and perfect commanders in the service of their country. They would not then, if they were trusted with fair and hopeful armies, suffer them, for want of just and wise discipline, to shed away from about them like sick feathers, though they be never so oft supplied; they would not suffer their empty and unrecruitable colonels of twenty men in a company to quaff out or convey into secret hoards the wages of a delusive list and a miserable remnant, yet in the meanwhile to be overmastered with a score or two of drunkards, the only soldiery left about them, or else to comply with all rapines and violences. No, certainly, if they knew aught of that knowledge that belongs to good men or good governors, they would not suffer these things.

But to return to our own institute : besides these constant exercises at home, there is another opportunity of gaining experience to be won from pleasure itself abroad; in those vernal seasons of the year when the air is calm and pleasant, it were an injury and sullenness against nature not to go out and see her riches, and partake in her rejoicing with heaven and earth. I should not therefore be a persuader to them of studying much then, after two or three years that they have well laid their grounds, but to ride out in companies, with prudent and safe guides, to all the quarters of the land, learning and observing all places of strength, all commodities of building and of soil for towns and tillage, harbours and ports for trade : sometimes taking sea as far as to our navy, to learn there also what they can in the practical knowledge of sailing and of sea-fight.

These ways would try all their peculiar gifts of nature ; and if there were any secret excellence among them would fetch it out, and give it fair opportunities to advance itself by, which could not but mightily redound to the good of this nation, and bring into fashion again those old admired virtues and excellencies, with far more advantage now in this purity of Christian knowledge. Nor shall we then need the monsieurs of Paris to take our hopeful youth into their slight and prodigal custodies, and send them over back again transformed into mimics, apes, and kickshaws. But if they desire to see other countries at three or four and twenty years of age, not to learn principles, but to enlarge experience and make wise observation, they will by that time be such as shall deserve the regard and honour of all men where they pass, and the society and friendship of those in all places who are best and most eminent. And perhaps then other nations will be glad to visit us for their breeding, or else to imitate us in their own country.

Now, lastly, for their diet there cannot be much
to say, save only that it would be best in the same
house ; for much time else would be lost abroad,
and many ill habits got ; and that it should be
plain, healthful, and moderate, I suppose is out of
controversy. Thus, Mr. Hartlib, you have a general view in writing, as your desire was, of that
which at several times I had discoursed with you
concerning the best and noblest way of education ;
not beginning, as some have done, from the cradle,
which yet might be worth many considerations, if
brevity had not been my scope ; many other circumstances also I could have mentioned, but this,
to such as have the worth in them to make trial,
for light and direction may be enough. Only I
believe that this is not a bow for every man to
shoot in that counts himself a teacher, but will
require sinews almost equal to those which Homer
gave Ulysses ; yet I am withal persuaded that it
may prove much more easy in the assay than it
now seems at a distance, and much more illustrious ;
howbeit not more difficult than I imagine, and
that imagination presents me with nothing but
very happy, and very possible according to best
wishes ; if God have so decreed, and this age
have spirit and capacity enough to apprehend.

AREOPAGITICA

A SPEECH FOR THE LIBERTY OF
UNLICENSED PRINTING TO THE
PARLIAMENT OF ENGLAND. 1644.

Τοὐλεύθερον δ' ἐκεῖνο· τίς θέλει πόλει
Χρηστόν τι βούλευμ' εἰς μέσον φέρειν ἔχων;
Καὶ ταῦθ' ὁ χρῄζων λαμπρός ἐσθ', ὁ μὴ θέλων
Σιγᾷ· τί τούτων ἐστ' ἰσαίτερον πόλει;—*Euripides.*

This is true liberty, when free-born men,
Having to advise the public, may speak free,
Which he who can, and will, deserves high praise;
Who neither can, nor will, may hold his peace:
What can be juster in a state than this?

THEY who to states and governors of the commonwealth direct their speech, high court of parliament, or wanting such access in a private condition, write that which they foresee may advance the public good; I suppose them, as at the beginning of no mean endeavour, not a little altered and moved inwardly in their minds; some with doubt of what will be the success, others with fear of what will be the censure; some with hope, others with confidence of what they have to speak. And me perhaps each of these dispositions, as the subject was whereon I entered, may have at other times variously affected; and likely might in these foremost expressions now also disclose which of them swayed most, but that the very attempt of this address thus made, and the thought of whom it hath recourse to, hath got the power within me to a passion, far more welcome than incidental to a preface.

Which though I stay not to confess ere any ask, I shall be blameless, if it be no other than the joy and gratulation which it brings to all who wish to promote their country's liberty; whereof this whole

discourse proposed will be a certain testimony, if
not a trophy. For this is not the liberty which
we can hope, that no grievance ever should arise
in the commonwealth; that let no man in this
world expect; but when complaints are freely
heard, deeply considered, and speedily reformed,
then is the utmost bound of civil liberty obtained
that wise men look for. To which if I now manifest, by the very sound of this which I shall utter,
that we are already in good part arrived, and yet
from such a steep disadvantage of tyranny and
superstition grounded into our principles as was
beyond the manhood of a Roman recovery, it will
be attributed first, as is most due, to the strong
assistance of God, our deliverer; next, to your
faithful guidance and undaunted wisdom, lords and
commons of England. Neither is it in God's esteem the diminution of his glory when honourable things are spoken of good men and worthy
magistrates; which if I now first should begin to
do, after so fair a progress of your laudable deeds,
and such a long obligement upon the whole realm
to your indefatigable virtues, I might be justly
reckoned among the tardiest and the unwillingest
of them that praise ye.

Nevertheless there being three principal things
without which all praising is but courtship and
flattery: first, when that only is praised which is
solidly worth praise; next, when greatest likeli-
hoods are brought that such things are truly and
really in those persons to whom they are ascribed;

the other, when he who praises, by shewing that
such his actual persuasion is of whom he writes, can
demonstrate that he flatters not ; the former two
of these I have heretofore endeavoured, rescuing
the employment from him who went about to im-
pair your merits with a trivial and malignant enco-
mium ; the latter as belonging chiefly to mine own
acquittal, that whom I so extolled I did not flatter,
hath been reserved opportunely to this occasion.
For he who freely magnifies what hath been nobly
done, and fears not to declare as freely what might be
done better, gives ye the best covenant of his fidelity;
and that his loyalest affection and his hope waits on
your proceedings. His highest praising is not flattery, and his plainest advice is a kind of praising ; for
though I should affirm and hold by argument that
it would fare better with truth, with learning, and
the commonwealth, if one of your published orders,
which I should name, were called in ; yet at the
same time it could not but much redound to the
lustre of your mild and equal government, whenas
private persons are hereby animated to think ye
better pleased with public advice than other statists
have been delighted heretofore with public flattery.
And men will then see what difference there is
between the magnanimity of a triennial parliament
and that jealous haughtiness of prelates and cabin
counsellors that usurped of late, whenas they shall
observe ye in the midst of your victories and suc-
cesses more gently brooking written exceptions
against a voted order than other courts, which had

9

produced nothing worth memory but the weak ostentation of wealth, would have endured the least signified dislike at any sudden proclamation.

If I should thus far presume upon the meek demeanour of your civil and gentle greatness, lords and commons, as what your published order hath directly said, that to gainsay, I might defend my- self with case, if any should accuse me of being new or insolent, did they but know how much better I find ye esteem it to imitate the old and ele- gant humanity of Greece than the barbaric pride of a Hunnish and Norwegian stateliness. And out of those ages to whose polite wisdom and letters we owe that we are not yet Goths and Jutlanders, I could name him who from his private house wrote that discourse to the parliament of Athens that persuades them to change the form of democracy which was then established. Such honour was done in those days to men who professed the study of wisdom and eloquence, not only in their own country but in other lands, that cities and signiories heard them gladly, and with great respect, if they had aught in public to admonish the state. Thus did Dion Prusæus, a stranger and a private orator, counsel the Rhodians against a former edict; and I abound with other like examples, which to set here would be superfluous. But if from the indus- try of a life wholly dedicated to studious labours, and those natural endowments haply not the worst for two and fifty degrees of northern latitude, so much must be derogated as to count me not equal to any of those who had this privilege, I would obtain to be thought not so inferior as yourselves are superior to the most of them who received their counsel ; and how far you excel them, be assured, lords and commons, there can no greater testimony appear than when your prudent spirit acknowledges and obeys the voice of reason, from what quarter soever it be heard speaking ; and renders ye as willing to repeat any act of your own setting forth as any set forth by your predecessors.

If ye be thus resolved, as it were injury to think ye were not, I know not what should withhold me from presenting ye with a fit instance wherein to shew both that love of truth which ye eminently profess, and that uprightness of your judgment which is not wont to be partial to yourselves ; by judging over again that order which ye have ordained 'to regulate printing: that no book, 'pamphlet, or paper shall be henceforth printed, 'unless the same be first approved and licensed 'by such, or at least one of such, as shall be thereto 'appointed.' For that part which preserves justly every man's copy to himself, or provides for the poor, I touch not ; only wish they be not made pretences to abuse and persecute honest and painful men who offend not in either of these particulars. But that other clause of licensing books, which we thought had died with his brother quadragesimal and matrimonial when the prelates expired, I shall now attend with such a homily as shall lay before ye, first, the inventors of it to be those whom ye will be

loath to own ; next, what is to be thought in general
of reading, whatever sort the books be; and that this
order avails nothing to the suppressing of scandalous, seditious, and libellous books, which were
mainly intended to be suppressed. Last, that it will
be primely to the discouragement of all learning, and
the stop of truth, not only by disexercising and blunt-
ing our abilities in what we know already, but by
hindering and cropping the discovery that might be
yet further made, both in religious and civil wisdom.

I deny not but that it is of greatest concernment
in the church and commonwealth to have a
vigilant eye how books demean themselves, as
well as men ; and thereafter to confine, imprison,
and do sharpest justice on them as malefactors ;
for books are not absolutely dead things, but do
contain a progeny of life in them to be as active as
that soul was whose progeny they are; nay, they
do preserve as in a vial the purest efficacy and
extraction of that living intellect that bred them.
I know they are as lively, and as vigorously pro-
ductive, as those fabulous dragon's teeth : and
being sown up and down, may chance to spring
up armed men. And yet, on the other hand,
unless wariness be used, as good almost kill a man
as kill a good book : who kills a man kills a
reasonable creature, God's image ; but he who
destroys a good book, kills reason itself, kills the
image of God, as it were, in the eye. Many a man
lives a burden to the earth ; but a good book is
the precious life-blood of a master-spirit, embalmed

and treasured up on purpose to a life beyond life.
It is true, no age can restore a life, whereof,
perhaps, there is no great loss ; and revolutions of
ages do not oft recover the loss of a rejected truth,
for the want of which whole nations fare the worse.
We should be wary, therefore, what persecution
we raise against the living labours of public men,
how we spill that seasoned life of man, preserved
and stored up in books ; since we see a kind of
homicide may be thus committed, sometimes a
martyrdom ; and if it extend to the whole impression, a kind of massacre, whereof the execution
ends not in the slaying of an elemental life, but
strikes at the ethereal and fifth essence, the breath
of reason itself ; slays an immortality rather than a
life. But lest I should be condemned of intro-
ducing licence while I oppose licensing, I refuse
not the pains to be so much historical as will serve
to shew what hath been done by ancient and
famous commonwealths against this disorder, till
the very time that this project of licensing crept
out of the inquisition, was catched up by our
prelates, and hath caught some of our presbyters.

In Athens, where books and wits were ever busier
than in any other part of Greece, I find but only
two sorts of writings which the magistrate cared to
take notice of ; those either blasphemous and
atheistical, or libellous. Thus the books of Pro-
tagoras were by the judges of Areopagus commanded to be burnt, and himself banished the
territory for a discourse begun with his confessing

not to know ' whether there were gods, or whether
'not.' And against defaming, it was agreed that
none should be traduced by name, as was the
manner of Vetus Comœdia, whereby we may guess
how they censured libelling ; and this course was
quick enough, as Cicero writes, to quell both the
desperate wits of other atheists, and the open way
of defaming, as the event showed. Of other sects
and opinions, though tending to voluptuousness,
and the denying of divine Providence, they took no
heed. Therefore we do not read that either
Epicurus, or that libertine school of Cyrene, or
what the Cynic impudence uttered, was ever ques-
tioned by the laws. Neither is it recorded that
the writings of those old comedians were suppressed, though the acting of them were forbid ;
and that Plato commended the reading of Aristophanes, the loosest of them all, to his royal
scholar Dionysius, is commonly known, and may
be excused, if holy Chrysostom, as is reported,
nightly studied so much the same author, and had
the art to cleanse a scurrilous vehemence into the
style of a rousing sermon.

That other leading city of Greece, Lacedæmon,
considering that Lycurgus their lawgiver was so
addicted to elegant learning as to have been the
first that brought out of Ionia the scattered works
of Homer, and sent the poet Thales from Crete, to
prepare and mollify the Spartan surliness with his
smooth songs and odes, the better to plant among
them law and civility ; it is to be wondered how

museless and unbookish they were, minding nought but the feats of war. There needed no licensing of books among them, for they disliked all but their own laconic apophthegms, and took a slight occasion to chase Archilochus out of their city, perhaps for composing in a higher strain than their own soldiery ballads and roundels could reach to ; or if it were for his broad verses, they were not therein so cautious but they were as dissolute in their promiscuous conversing ; whence Euripides affirms, in Andromache, that their women were all unchaste.

This much may give us light after what sort of books were prohibited among the Greeks. The Romans also for many ages trained up only to a military roughness, resembling most the Lacedæ-monian guise, knew of learning little but what their twelve tables and the pontific college with their augurs and flamens taught them in religion and law ; so unacquainted with other learning that when Carneades and Critolaus, with the stoic Diogenes, coming ambassadors to Rome, took thereby occasion to give the city a taste of their philosophy, they were suspected for seducers by no less a man than Cato the Censor, who moved it in the senate to dismiss them speedily, and to banish all such Attic babblers out of Italy. But Scipio and others of the noblest senators withstood him and his old Sabine austerity ; honoured and ad-mired the men ; and the censor himself at last, in his old age, fell to the study of that whereof before he was so scrupulous. And yet, at the same time, Nævius and Plautus, the first Latin comedians, had filled the city with all the borrowed scenes of Menander and Philemon. Then began to be considered there also what was to be done to libellous books and authors; for Nævius was quickly cast into prison for his unbridled pen, and released by the tribunes upon his recantation : we read also that libels were burnt, and the makers punished, by Augustus.

The like severity, no doubt, was used, if aught were impiously written against their esteemed gods. Except in these two points, how the world went in books the magistrate kept no reckoning. And therefore Lucretius, without impeachment, versifies his Epicurism to Memmius, and had the honour to be set forth the second time by Cicero, so great a father of the commonwealth ; although himself disputes against that opinion in his own writings. Nor was the satirical sharpness or naked plainness of Lucilius, or Catullus, or Flaccus, by any order prohibited. And for matters of state, the story of Titus Livius, though it extolled that part which Pompey held, was not therefore suppressed by Octavius Cæsar, of the other faction. But that Naso was by him banished in his old age for the wanton poems of his youth, was but a mere covert of state over some secret cause ; and besides, the books were neither banished nor called in. From hence we shall meet with little else but tyranny in the Roman empire, that we may not marvel if not so often bad as good books were silenced. I shall therefore deem to have been large enough, in producing what among the ancients was punishable to write, save only which, all other arguments were free to treat on.

By this time the emperors were become Christians, whose discipline in this point I do not find to have been more severe than was formerly in practice. The books of those whom they took to be grand heretics were examined, refuted, and condemned in the general councils; and not till then were prohibited, or burnt, by authority of the emperor. As for the writings of heathen authors, unless they were plain invectives against Christianity, as those of Porphyrius and Proclus, they met with no interdict that can be cited, till about the year 400, in a Carthaginian council, wherein bishops themselves were forbid to read the books of Gentiles, but heresies they might read; while others long before them, on the contrary, scrupled more the books of heretics than of Gentiles. And that the primitive councils and bishops were wont only to declare what books were not commendable, passing no further, but leaving it to each one's conscience to read or to lay by, till after the year 800, is observed already by Padre Paolo, the great unmasker of the Trentine council. After which time the popes of Rome, engrossing what they pleased of political rule into their own hands, extended their dominion over men's eyes, as they had before over their judgments, burning and

prohibiting to be read what they fancied not ; yet
sparing in their censures, and the books not many
which they so dealt with; till Martin the Fifth, by
his bull, not only prohibited, but was the first that
excommunicated the reading of heretical books ;
for about that time Wicklef and Husse growing
terrible were they who first drove the papal court
to a stricter policy of prohibiting. Which course
Leo the Tenth and his successors followed, until
the council of Trent and the Spanish inquisition,
engendering together, brought forth or perfected
those catalogues and expurging indexes that rake
through the entrails of many an old good author
with a violation worse than any could be offered to
his tomb.

Nor did they stay in matters heretical, but any
subject that was not to their palate, they either
condemned in a prohibition, or had it straight into
the new purgatory of an index. To fill up the
measure of encroachment, their last invention was
to ordain that no book, pamphlet, or paper should
be printed (as if St. Peter had bequeathed them the
keys of the press also as well as of Paradise) unless
it were approved and licensed under the hands of
two or three gluttonous friars. For example :—

‘ Let the chancellor Cini be pleased to see if in this pre-
‘ sent work be contained aught that may withstand the
‘ printing.
‘ Vincent Rabatta, Vicar of Florence.’

‘ I have seen this present work, and find nothing athwart
‘ the Catholic faith and good manners : in witness
‘ whereof I have given, &c.
‘ Nicolò Cini, Chancellor of Florence.’

'Attending the precedent relation, it is allowed that this
 'present work of Davanzati may be printed.
                               'Vincent Rabatta,' &c.

'It may be printed, July 15.
 'Friar Simon Mompei d'Amelia, Chancellor of the
                               'Holy Office in Florence.'

Sure they have a conceit, if he of the bottomless
pit had not long since broke prison, that this
quadruple exorcism would bar him down.   I fear
their next design will be to get into their custody
the licensing of that which they say Claudius intended, but went not through with.   Vouchsafe to
see another of their forms, the Roman stamp :—

'Imprimatur, If it seem good to the reverend master of
 'the Holy Palace.
                               'Belcastro, Vicegerent.'
'Imprimatur,
    'Friar Nicolò Rodolphi, Master of the Holy Palace.'

Sometimes five imprimaturs are seen together,
dialogue wise, in the piazza of one titlepage, com-
plimenting and ducking each to other with their
shaven reverences, whether the author, who stands
by in perplexity at the foot of his epistle, shall to
the press or to the sponge.   These are the pretty
responsories, these are the dear antiphonies, that
so bewitched of late our prelates and their chaplains with the goodly echo they made ; and besotted us to the gay imitation of a lordly imprimatur, one from Lambeth-house, another from the
west end of Paul's ; so apishly romanizing, that
the word of command still was set down in Latin ;
as if the learned grammatical pen that wrote it
would cast no ink without Latin ; or perhaps, as
they thought, because no vulgar tongue was worthy

to express the pure conceit of an imprimatur; but rather, as I hope, for that our English, the language of men ever famous and foremost in the achievements of liberty, will not easily find servile letters enow to spell such a dictatory presumption Englished.

And thus ye have the inventors and the original of book licensing ripped up and drawn as lineally as any pedigree. We have it not, that can be heard of, from any ancient state, or polity, or church, nor by any statute left us by our ancestors elder or later; nor from the modern custom of any reformed city or church abroad; but from the most anti-christian council, and the most tyrannous inquisition that ever inquired. Till then books were ever as freely admitted into the world as any other birth; the issue of the brain was no more stifled than the issue of the womb: no envious Juno sat cross-legged over the nativity of any man's intellectual offspring; but if it proved a monster, who denies but that it was justly burnt, or sunk into the sea? But that a book, in worse condition than a peccant soul, should be to stand before a jury ere it be born to the world, and undergo yet in darkness the judgment of Radamanth and his colleagues, ere it can pass the ferry backward into light, was never heard before, till that mysterious iniquity, provoked and troubled at the first entrance of reformation, sought out new limboes and new hells wherein they might include our books also within the number of their damned. And this was the rare morsel so officiously snatched up and so illfavouredly imitated by our inquisiturient bishops, and the attendant minorites, their chaplains. That ye like not now these most certain authors of this licensing order, and that all sinister intention was far distant from your thoughts when ye were importuned the passing it, all men who know the integrity of your actions, and how ye honour truth, will clear ye readily.

But some will say, what though the inventors were bad, the thing for all that may be good. It may be so; yet if that thing be no such deep invention, but obvious and easy for any man to light on, and yet best and wisest commonwealths through all ages and occasions have forborne to use it, and falsest seducers and oppressors of men were the first who took it up, and to no other purpose but to obstruct and hinder the first approach of reformation; I am of those who believe, it will be a harder alchymy than Lullius ever knew, to sublimate any good use out of such an invention. Yet this only is what I request to gain from this reason, that it may be held a dangerous and suspicious fruit, as certainly it deserves, for the tree that bore it, until I can dissect one by one the properties it has. But I have first to finish, as was propounded, what is to be thought in general of reading books, whatever sort they be, and whether be more the benefit or the harm that thence proceeds.

Not to insist upon the examples of Moses, Daniel, and Paul, who were skilful in all the

learning of the Egyptians, Chaldeans, and Greeks,
which could not probably be without reading their
books of all sorts, in Paul especially, who thought
it no defilement to insert into holy scripture the
sentences of three Greek poets, and one of them a
tragedian; the question was notwithstanding sometimes controverted among the primitive doctors,
but with great odds on that side which affirmed it
both lawful and profitable, as was then evidently
perceived, when Julian the Apostate, and subtlest
enemy to our faith, made a decree forbidding
Christians the study of heathen learning; for, said
he, they wound us with our own weapons, and
with our own arts and sciences they overcome us.
And indeed the Christians were put so to their
shifts by this crafty means, and so much in danger
to decline into all ignorance, that the two Apolli-
narii were fain, as a man may say, to coin all the
seven liberal sciences out of the Bible, reducing it
into divers forms of orations, poems, dialogues,
even to the calculating of a new Christian grammar.

But, saith the historian Socrates, the providence
of God provided better than the industry of Apol-
linarius and his son, by taking away that illiterate
law with the life of him who devised it. So great
an injury they then held it to be deprived of
Hellenic learning; and thought it a persecution
more undermining and secretly decaying the
church than the open cruelty of Decius or Diocle-
tian. And perhaps it was with the same politic
drift that the devil whipt St. Jerome in a lenten

dream, for reading **Cicero**; or else it was a phan-
tasm, bred by the fever which had then seized him.
For had an angel been his discipliner, unless it
were for dwelling too much on Ciceronianisms,
and had chastised the reading, not the vanity, it had
been plainly partial, first, to correct him for grave
Cicero, and not for scurril Plautus, whom he confesses to have been reading not long before; next
to correct him only, and let so many more ancient
fathers wax old in those pleasant and florid studies,
without the lash of such a tutoring apparition;
insomuch that Basil teaches how some good use
may be made of Margites, a sportful poem, not now
extant, writ by Homer; and why not then of Mor-
gante, an Italian romance much to the same purpose?

But if it be agreed we shall be tried by visions,
there is a vision recorded by Eusebius, far an-
cienter than this tale of Jerome, to the nun Eusto-
chium, and besides, has nothing of a fever in it.
Dionysius Alexandrinus was, about the year 240, a
person of great name in the church for piety and
learning, who had wont to avail himself much
against heretics, by being conversant in their books;
until a certain presbyter laid it scrupulously to his
conscience, how he durst venture himself among
those defiling volumes. The worthy man, loath
to give offence, fell into a new debate with himself,
what was to be thought; when suddenly a vision
sent from God (it is his own epistle that so avers
it) confirmed him in these words: 'Read any
'books whatever come to thy hands, for thou art

'sufficient both to judge aright and to examine
'each matter.' To this revelation he assented the
sooner, as he confesses, because it was answerable
to that of the apostle to the Thessalonians :
'Prove all things, hold fast that which is good.'

And he might have added another remarkable
saying of the same author : 'To the pure, all things
'are pure ;' not only meats and drinks, but all kind
of knowledge, whether of good or evil : the knowledge cannot defile, nor consequently the books, if
the will and conscience be not defiled.   For books
are as meat and viands are ; some of good, some of
evil substance ; and yet God in that unapocryphal
vision said without exception, 'Rise, Peter, kill
'and eat ;' leaving the choice to each man's discretion.   Wholesome meats to a vitiated stomach
differ little or nothing from unwholesome; and best
books to a naughty mind are not unapplicable to
occasions of evil. Bad meats will scarce breed
good nourishment in the healthiest concoction ;
but herein the difference is of bad books, that they
to a discreet and judicious reader serve in many
respects to discover, to confute, to forewarn, and to
illustrate.   Whereof what better witness can ye expect I should produce, than one of your own now
sitting in parliament, the chief of learned men reputed in this land, Mr. Selden ; whose volume of
natural and national laws proves, not only by great
authorities brought together, but by exquisite reasons and theorems almost mathematically demon-
strative, that all opinions, yea, errors, known, read,

and collated, are of main service and assistance toward the speedy attainment of what is truest.

I conceive, therefore, that when God did enlarge the universal diet of man's body, (saving ever the rules of temperance,) he then also, as before, left arbitrary the dieting and repasting of our minds ; as wherein every mature man might have to exercise his own leading capacity. How great a virtue is temperance, how much of moment through the whole life of man ! Yet God commits the managing so great a trust, without particular law or prescription, wholly to the demeanour of every grown man. And therefore when he himself tabled the Jews from heaven, that omer, which was every man's daily portion of manna, is computed to have been more than might have well sufficed the heartiest feeder thrice as many meals. For those actions which enter into a man, rather than issue out of him, and therefore defile not, God uses not to captivate ✝ under a perpetual childhood of prescription, but trusts him with the gift of reason to be his own chooser ; there were but little work left for preaching, if law and compulsion should grow so fast upon those things which heretofore were governed only by exhortation. Solomon informs us that much reading is a weariness to the flesh ; but neither he nor other inspired author tells us that such or such reading is unlawful ; yet certainly had God thought good to limit us herein, it had been much more expedient to have told us what was unlawful than what was wearisome.

As for the burning of those Ephesian books by
St. Paul's converts; it is replied, the books were
magic, the Syriac so renders them. It was a
private act, a voluntary act, and leaves us to a
voluntary imitation : the men in remorse burnt
those books which were their own ; the magistrate
by this example is not appointed ; these men
practised the books, another might perhaps have
read them in some sort usefully. Good and evil
we know in the field of this world grow up together almost inseparably ; and the knowledge of
good is so involved and interwoven with the knowledge of evil, and in so many cunning resemblances
hardly to be discerned, that those confused seeds
which were imposed upon Psyche as an incessant
labour to cull out and sort asunder, were not more
intermixed. It was from out the rind of one apple
tasted that the knowledge of good and evil, as
two twins cleaving together, leaped forth into the
world. And perhaps this is that doom which
Adam fell into of knowing good and evil ; that is
to say, of knowing good by evil.

As therefore the state of man now is, what wisdom can there be to choose, what continence to
forbear, without the knowledge of evil ? He that
can apprehend and consider vice with all her baits
and seeming pleasures, and yet abstain, and yet distinguish, and yet prefer that which is truly better,
he is the true warfaring Christian. I cannot praise
a fugitive and cloistered virtue unexercised and
unbreathed, that never sallies out and seeks her

adversary, but slinks out of the race, where that immortal garland is to be run for, not without dust and
heat. Assuredly we bring not innocence into the
world, we bring impurity much rather ; that which
purifies us is trial, and trial is by what is contrary.
That virtue therefore which is but a youngling in the
contemplation of evil, and knows not the utmost
that vice promises to her followers, and rejects it,
is but a blank virtue, not a pure ; her whiteness is
but an excremental whiteness ; which was the reason
why our sage and serious poet Spenser, (whom I dare
be known to think a better teacher than Scotus or
Aquinas,) describing true temperance under the
person of Guion, brings him in with his palmer
through the cave of Mammon, and the bower of
earthly bliss, that he might see and know, and yet
abstain.

Since therefore the knowledge and survey of vice
is in this world so necessary to the constituting
of human virtue, and the scanning of error to the
confirmation of truth, how can we more safely, and
with less danger, scout into the regions of sin and
falsity, than by reading all manner of tractates,
and hearing all manner of reason ? And this is the
benefit which may be had of books promiscuously
read. But of the harm that may result hence,
three kinds are usually reckoned. First, is feared
the infection that may spread ; but then, all human
learning and controversy in religious points must
remove out of the world, yea, the Bible itself ; for
that ofttimes relates blasphemy not nicely, it de-

scribes the carnal sense of wicked men not un-
elegantly, it brings in holiest men passionately
murmuring against Providence through all the
arguments of Epicurus : in other great disputes it
answers dubiously and darkly to the common
reader ; and ask a Talmudist what ails the modesty
of his marginal Keri, that Moses and all the prophets cannot persuade him to pronounce the textual
Chetiv.   For these causes we all know the Bible
itself put by the papist into the first rank of prohibited books.   The ancientest fathers must be next
removed, as Clement of Alexandria, and that
Eusebian book of evangelic preparation, transmit-
ting our ears through a hoard of heathenish ob-
scenities to receive the gospel.   Who finds not that
Irenæus, Epiphanius, Jerome, and others discover
more heresies than they well confute, and that oft
for heresy which is the truer opinion ?

Nor boots it to say for these, and all the heathen
writers of greatest infection, if it must be thought
so, with whom is bound up the life of human
learning, that they wrote in an unknown tongue,
so long as we are sure those languages are known
as well to the worst of men, who are both most
able and most diligent to instil the poison they
suck, first into the courts of princes, acquainting
them with the choicest delights, and criticisms of
sin.   As perhaps did that Petronius, whom Nero
called his arbiter, the master of his revels ; and that
notorious ribald of Arezzo, dreaded and yet dear to
the Italian courtiers.   I name not him, for pos-

terity's sake, whom Henry the Eighth named in
merriment his vicar of hell. By which compendious way all the contagion that foreign books can
infuse will find a passage to the people far easier
and shorter than an Indian voyage, though it could
be sailed either by the north of Cataio eastward or
of Canada westward, while our Spanish licensing
gags the English press never so severely.

But, on the other side, that infection which is
from books of controversy in religion is more
doubtful and dangerous to the learned than to the
ignorant ; and yet those books must be permitted
untouched by the licenser. It will be hard to
instance where any ignorant man hath been ever
seduced by any papistical book in English, unless
it were commended and expounded to him by some
of that clergy ; and indeed all such tractates,
whether false or true, are as the prophecy of Isaiah
was to the eunuch, not to be understood without
a guide. But of our priests and doctors how
many have been corrupted by studying the com-
ments of Jesuits and Sorbonists, and how fast they
could transfuse that corruption into the people, our
experience is both late and sad. It is not forgot
since the acute and distinct Arminius was perverted
merely by the perusing of a nameless discourse
written at Delft, which at first he took in hand to
confute.

Seeing therefore that those books, and those in
great abundance, which are likeliest to taint both
life and doctrine, cannot be suppressed without the

fall of learning and of all ability in disputation, and that these books of either sort are most and soonest catching to the learned, (from whom to the common people whatever is heretical or dissolute may quickly be conveyed,) and that evil manners are as perfectly learnt without books a thousand other ways which cannot be stopped, and evil doctrine not with books can propagate, except a teacher guide, which he might also do without writing, and so beyond prohibiting; I am not able to unfold how this cautelous enterprise of licensing can be exempted from the number of vain and impossible attempts. And he who were pleasantly disposed could not well avoid to liken it to the exploit of that gallant man who thought to pound up the crows by shutting his park gate.

Besides another inconvenience, if learned men be the first receivers out of books, and dispreaders both of vice and error, how shall the licensers themselves be confided in, unless we can confer upon them, or they assume to themselves, above all others in the land, the grace of infallibility and uncorruptedness? And again, if it be true that a wise man, like a good refiner, can gather gold out of the drossiest volume, and that a fool will be a fool with the best book, yea, or without book; there is no reason that we should deprive a wise man of any advantage to his wisdom, while we seek to restrain from a fool that which being restrained will be no hindrance to his folly. For if there should be so much exactness always used to keep that from him which is unfit for his reading, we should, in the judgment of Aristotle not only but of Solomon and of our Saviour, not vouchsafe him good precepts, and by consequence not willingly admit him to good books ; as being certain that a wise man will make better use of an idle pamphlet than a fool will do of sacred scripture.

It is next alleged, we must not expose ourselves to temptations without necessity, and next to that, not employ our time in vain things. To both these objections one answer will serve, out of the grounds already laid, that to all men such books are not temptations, nor vanities ; but useful drugs and materials wherewith to temper and compose effective and strong medicines, which man's life cannot want. The rest, as children and childish men, who have not the art to qualify and prepare these working minerals, well may be exhorted to forbear ; but hindered forcibly they cannot be, by all the licensing that sainted inquisition could ever yet contrive ; which is what I promised to deliver next : that this order of licensing conduces nothing to the end for which it was framed ; and hath almost prevented me by being clear already while thus much hath been explaining. See the ingenuity of Truth, who, when she gets a free and willing hand, opens herself faster than the pace of method and discourse can overtake her. It was the task which I began with, to shew that no nation, or well instituted state, if they valued books at all, did ever use this way of licensing ; and it might be

answered, that this is a piece of prudence lately
discovered.

To which I return, that as it was a thing slight
and obvious to think on, so if it had been difficult
to find out, there wanted not among them long
since who suggested such a course ; which they
not following leave us a pattern of their judgment
that it was not the not knowing, but the not
approving, which was the cause of their not using
it. Plato, a man of high authority indeed, but
least of all for his Commonwealth, in the book of
his laws, which no city ever yet received, fed his
fancy with making many edicts to his airy burgo-
masters, which they who otherwise admire him
wish had been rather buried and excused in the
genial cups of an academic night sitting. By which
laws he seems to tolerate no kind of learning, but
by unalterable decree, consisting most of practical
traditions, to the attainment whereof a library of
smaller bulk than his own dialogues would be
abundant. And there also enacts, that no poet
should so much as read to any private man what he
had written, until the judges and law keepers had
seen it and allowed it ; but that Plato meant this
law peculiarly to that commonwealth which he had
imagined, and to no other, is evident. Why was
he not else a lawgiver to himself, but a transgressor,
and to be expelled by his own magistrates, both
for the wanton epigrams and dialogues which he
made, and his perpetual reading of Sophron Mimus
and Aristophanes, books of grossest infamy ; and

also for commending the latter of them, though he were the malicious libeller of his chief friends, to be read by the tyrant Dionysius, who had little need of such trash to spend his time on? But that he knew this licensing of poems had reference and dependence to many other provisoes there set down in his fancied republic, which in this world could have no place; and so neither he himself, nor any magistrate or city, ever imitated that course, which, taken apart from those other collateral injunctions, must needs be vain and fruitless.

For if they fell upon one kind of strictness, unless their care were equal to regulate all other things of like aptness to corrupt the mind, that single endeavour they knew would be but a fond labour; to shut and fortify one gate against corruption, and be necessitated to leave others round about wide open. If we think to regulate printing, thereby to rectify manners, we must regulate all recreations and pastimes, all that is delightful to man. No music must be heard, no song be set or sung, but what is grave and Doric. There must be licensing dancers, that no gesture, motion, or deportment be taught our youth, but what by their allowance shall be thought honest; for such Plato was provided of. It will ask more than the work of twenty licensers to examine all the lutes, the violins, and the guitars in every house; they must not be suffered to prattle as they do, but must be licensed what they may say. And who shall silence all the airs and madrigals that whisper softness in chambers? The

windows also, and the balconies, must be thought
on; there are shrewd books with dangerous frontis-
pieces set to sale : who shall prohibit them, shall
twenty licensers? The villages also must have
their visitors to inquire what lectures the bagpipe
and the rebec reads, even to the ballatry and the
gamut of every municipal fiddler ; for these are the
countryman's Arcadias, and his Monte Mayors.

Next, what more national corruption, for which
England hears ill abroad, than household gluttony?
Who shall be the rectors of our daily rioting?
And what shall be done to inhibit the multitudes
that frequent those houses where drunkenness is
sold and harboured? Our garments also should
be referred to the licensing of some more sober
workmasters, to see them cut into a less wanton
garb. Who shall regulate all the mixed conversation of our youth, male and female together, as is
the fashion of this country? Who shall still appoint what shall be discoursed, what presumed,
and no further? Lastly, who shall forbid and
separate all idle resort, all evil company? These
things will be, and must be ; but how they shall be
least hurtful, how least enticing, herein consists
the grave and governing wisdom of a state.

To sequester out of the world into Atlantic and
Utopian politics, which never can be drawn into
use, will not mend our condition ; but to ordain
wisely as in this world of evil, in the midst whereof
God hath placed us unavoidably. Nor is it Plato's
licensing of books will do this, which necessarily

pulls along with it so many other kinds of licensing as will make us all both ridiculous and weary,
and yet frustrate ; but those unwritten, or at least
unconstraining laws of virtuous education, religious
and civil nurture, which Plato there mentions as
the bonds and ligaments of the commonwealth,
the pillars and the sustainers of every written statute ; these they be which will bear chief sway in
such matters as these, when all licensing will be
easily eluded. Impunity and remissness for certain
are the bane of a commonwealth ; but here the great
art lies, to discern in what the law is to bid restraint
and punishment, and in what things persuasion only
is to work. If every action which is good or evil in
man at ripe years were to be under pittance, prescription, and compulsion, what were virtue but a
name, what praise could be then due to well doing,
what gramercy to be sober, just, or continent ?

Many there be that complain of divine Providence for suffering Adam to transgress. Foolish
tongues ! when God gave him reason, he gave him
freedom to choose, for reason is but choosing ; he
had been else a mere artificial Adam, such an
Adam as he is in the motions.[1] We ourselves
esteem not of that obedience, or love, or gift,
which is of force ; God therefore left him free, set
before him a provoking object ever almost in his
eyes ; herein consisted his merit, herein the right
of his reward, the praise of his abstinence. Wherefore did he create passions within us, pleasures

[1] Puppet-shows.—ED.

round about us, but that these rightly tempered are the very ingredients of virtue? They are not skilful considerers of human things who imagine to remove sin by removing the matter of sin; for, besides that it is a huge heap increasing under the very act of diminishing, though some part of it may for a time be withdrawn from some persons, it cannot from all, in such a universal thing as books are; and when this is done, yet the sin remains entire. Though ye take from a covetous man all his treasure, he has yet one jewel left, ye cannot bereave him of his covetousness. Banish all objects of lust, shut up all youth into the severest discipline that can be exercised in any hermitage, ye cannot make them chaste that came not thither so : such great care and wisdom is required to the right managing of this point.

Suppose we could expel sin by this means; look how much we thus expel of sin, so much we expel of virtue : for the matter of them both is the same : remove that, and ye remove them both alike. This justifies the high providence of God, who, though he commands us temperance, justice, continence, yet pours out before us even to a profuseness all desirable things, and gives us minds that can wander beyond all limit and satiety. Why should we then affect a rigour contrary to the manner of God and of nature, by abridging or scanting those means, which books freely permitted are, both to the trial of virtue and the exercise of truth?

It would be better done, to learn that the law

must needs be frivolous which goes to restrain things uncertainly and yet equally working to good and to evil. And were I the chooser, a dram of well-doing should be preferred before many times as much the forcible hindrance of evil doing. For God sure esteems the growth and completing of one virtuous person more than the restraint of ten vicious. And albeit whatever thing we hear or see, sitting, walking, travelling, or conversing, may be fitly called our book, and is of the same effect that writings are ; yet grant the thing to be prohibited were only books, it appears that this order hitherto is far insufficient to the end which it intends. Do we not see, not once or oftener, but weekly, that continued court-libel [1] against the parliament and city, printed, as the wet sheets can witness, and dispersed among us for all that licensing can do? Yet this is the prime service, a man would think, wherein this order should give proof of itself. If it were executed, you will say. But certain, if execution be remiss or blindfold now, and in this particular, what will it be hereafter, and in other books?

If then the order shall not be vain and frustrate, behold a new labour, lords and commons, ye must repeal and proscribe all scandalous and unlicensed books already printed and divulged ; after ye have drawn them up into a list, that all may know which are condemned, and which not ; and ordain that no foreign books be delivered out of custody,

[1] The 'Mercurius Aulicus,' a royalist weekly paper.—ED.

till they have been read over.   This office will require the whole time of not a few overseers, and
those no vulgar men.   There be also books which
are partly useful and excellent, partly culpable and
pernicious ; this work will ask as many more
officials, to make expurgations and expunctions,
that the commonwealth of learning be not damni-
fied. In fine, when the multitude of books increase
upon their hands, ye must be fain to catalogue all
those printers who are found frequently offending,
and forbid the importation of their whole suspected
typography.   In a word, that this your order may
be exact, and not deficient, ye must reform it perfectly, according to the model of Trent and Sevil,
which I know ye abhor to do.

Yet though ye should condescend to this, which
God forbid, the order still would be but fruitless
and defective to that end whereto ye meant it. If
to prevent sects and schisms, who is so unread or
uncatechised in story that hath not heard of many
sects refusing books as a hindrance, and preserving their doctrine unmixed for many ages, only
by unwritten traditions? The Christian faith (for
that was once a schism) is not unknown to have
spread all over Asia ere any gospel or epistle
was seen in writing. If the amendment of manners be aimed at, look into Italy and Spain,
whether those places be one scruple the better, the
honester, the wiser, the chaster, since all the inquisi-
tional rigour that hath been executed upon books.

Another reason, whereby to make it plain that

this order will miss the end it seeks, consider by
the quality which ought to be in every licenser. It
cannot be denied, but that he who is made judge
to sit upon the birth or death of books, whether
they may be wafted into this world or not, had
need to be a man above the common measure,
both studious, learned, and judicious ; there may
be else no mean mistakes in the censure of what is
passable or not ; which is also no mean injury. If
he be of such worth as behoves him, there cannot
be a more tedious and unpleasing journeywork, a
greater loss of time levied upon his head, than to
be made the perpetual reader of unchosen books
and pamphlets, ofttimes huge volumes. There is
no book that is acceptable, unless at certain seasons ; but to be enjoined the reading of that at all
times, and in a hand scarce legible, whereof three
pages would not down at any time in the fairest
print, is an imposition I cannot believe how he
that values time, and his own studies, or is but of
a sensible nostril, should be able to endure. In
this one thing I crave leave of the present licensers
to be pardoned for so thinking : who doubtless
took this office up, looking on it through their
obedience to the parliament, whose command perhaps made all things seem easy and unlaborious to
them ; but that this short trial hath wearied them
out already, their own expressions and excuses to
them who make so many journeys to solicit their
licence, are testimony enough. Seeing therefore
those who now possess the employment by all

evident signs wish themselves well rid of it, and
that no man of worth, none that is not a plain un-
thrift of his own hours, is ever likely to succeed
them, except he mean to put himself to the salary
of a press corrector, we may easily foresee what
kind of licensers we are to expect hereafter, either
ignorant, imperious, and remiss, or basely pecu-
niary.   This is what I had to show, wherein this
order cannot conduce to that end whereof it bears
the intention.

I lastly proceed from the no good it can do, to
the manifest hurt it causes, in being first the
greatest discouragement and affront that can be
offered to learning and to learned men.   It was the
complaint and lamentation of prelates, upon every
least of a motion to remove pluralities and distri-
bute more equally church revenues, that then all
learning would be for ever dashed and discouraged.
But as for that opinion, I never found cause to
think that the tenth part of learning stood or fell
with the clergy : nor could I ever but hold it for a
sordid and unworthy speech of any churchman
who had a competency left him.   If therefore ye
be loath to dishearten utterly and discontent, not
the mercenary crew of false pretenders to learning,
but the free and ingenuous sort of such as evidently
were born to study and love learning for itself, not
for lucre, or any other end, but the service of God
and of truth, and perhaps that lasting fame and
perpetuity of praise, which God and good men
have consented shall be the reward of those whose

published labours advance the good of mankind : then know, that so far to distrust the judgment and the honesty of one who hath but a common repute in learning, and never yet offended, as not to count him fit to print his mind without a tutor and examiner, lest he should drop a schism, or something of corruption, is the greatest displeasure and indignity to a free and knowing spirit that can be put upon him.

What advantage is it to be a man over it is to be a boy at school, if we have only escaped the ferula to come under the fescue of an imprimatur? if serious and elaborate writings, as if they were no more than the theme of a grammar-lad under his pedagogue, must not be uttered without the cursory eyes of a temporizing and extemporizing licenser? He who is not trusted with his own actions, his drift not being known to be evil, and standing to the hazard of law and penalty, has no great argument to think himself reputed in the commonwealth wherein he was born for other than a fool or a foreigner. When a man writes to the world, he summons up all his reason and deliberation to assist him ; he searches, meditates, is industrious, and likely consults and confers with his judicious friends ; after all which done, he takes himself to be informed in what he writes as well as any that wrote before him ; if in this, the most consummate act of his fidelity and ripeness, no years, no industry, no former proof of his abilities, can bring him to that state of maturity as not to be still

11

mistrusted and suspected, unless he carry all his considerate diligence, all his midnight watchings, and expense of Palladian oil, to the hasty view of an unleisured licenser, perhaps much his younger, perhaps far his inferior in judgment, perhaps one who never knew the labour of bookwriting; and if he be not repulsed, or slighted, must appear in print like a puny with his guardian, and his censor's hand on the back of his title to be his bail and surety that he is no idiot or seducer; it cannot be but a dishonour and derogation to the author, to the book, to the privilege and dignity of learning.

And what if the author shall be one so copious of fancy as to have many things well worth the adding come into his mind after licensing, while the book is yet under the press, which not seldom happens to the best and diligentest writers; and that perhaps a dozen times in one book. The printer dares not go beyond his licensed copy; so often then must the author trudge to his leave-giver, that those his new insertions may be viewed; and many a jaunt will be made, ere that licenser, for it must be the same man, can either be found, or found at leisure; meanwhile either the press must stand still, which is no small damage, or the author lose his accuratest thoughts, and send the book forth worse than he had made it, which to a diligent writer is the greatest melancholy and vexation that can befall.

And how can a man teach with authority, which is the life of teaching; how can he be a doctor in

his book, as he ought to be, or else had better be
silent, whenas all he teaches, all he delivers, is but
under the tuition, under the correction of his
patriarchal licenser, to blot or alter what precisely
accords not with the hide-bound humour which he
calls his judgment ? When every acute reader, upon
the first sight of a pedantic licence, will be ready
with these like words to ding the book a quoit's
distance from him :—'I hate a pupil teacher ; I
' endure not an instructor that comes to me under
' the wardship of an overseeing fist. I know nothing
' of the licenser, but that I have his own hand here
' for his arrogance ; who shall warrant me his
' judgment ?' ' The state, sir,' replies the stationer :
but has a quick return :—' The state shall be my
' governors, but not my critics ; they may be mis-
' taken in the choice of a licenser, as easily as this
' license may be mistaken in an author. This is some
' common stuff :' and he might add from Sir Francis
Bacon, that 'such authorized books are but the
' language of the times.' For though a licenser
should happen to be judicious more than ordinary,
which will be a great jeopardy of the next succession,
yet his very office and his commission enjoins him to
let pass nothing but what is vulgarly received already.

Nay, which is more lamentable, if the work of
any deceased author, though never so famous in his
lifetime, and even to this day, comes to their hands
for licence to be printed, or reprinted, if there be
found in his book one sentence of a venturous edge,
uttered in the height of zeal, (and who knows

whether it might not be the dictate of a divine spirit?) yet not suiting with every low decrepit humour of their own, though it were Knox himself, the reformer of a kingdom, that spake it, they will not pardon him their dash;[1] the sense of that great man shall to all posterity be lost, for the fearfulness or the presumptuous rashness of a perfunctory licenser. And to what an author this violence hath been lately done, and in what book, of greatest consequence to be faithfully published, I could now instance, but shall forbear till a more convenient season. Yet if these things be not resented seriously and timely by them who have the remedy in their power, but that such ironmoulds as these shall have authority to gnaw out the choicest periods of exquisitest books, and to commit such a treacherous fraud against the orphan remainders of worthiest men after death, the more sorrow will belong to that hapless race of men whose misfortune it is to have understanding. Henceforth let no man care to learn, or care to be more than worldly wise; for certainly in higher matters to be ignorant and slothful, to be a common steadfast dunce, will be the only pleasant life, and only in request.

And as it is a particular disesteem of every knowing person alive, and most injurious to the written labours and monuments of the dead, so to me it seems an undervaluing and vilifying of the whole nation. I cannot set so light by all the invention, the art, the wit, the grave and solid judgment which

---

[1] Forego their erasure.—ED.

is in England, as that it can be comprehended in any twenty capacities, how good soever; much less that it should not pass except their superintendence be over it, except it be sifted and strained with their strainers, that it should be uncurrent without their mutual stamp. Truth and understanding are not such wares as to be monopolized and traded in by tickets, and statutes, and standards. We must not think to make a staple commodity of all the knowledge in the land, to mark and license it like our broad-cloth and our wool-packs. What is it but a servitude like that imposed by the Philistines, not to be allowed the sharpening of our own axes and coulters, but we must repair from all quarters to twenty licensing forges?

Had any one written and divulged erroneous things and scandalous to honest life, misusing and forfeiting the esteem had of his reason among men, if after conviction this only censure were adjudged him, that he should never henceforth write but what were first examined by an appointed officer, whose hand should be annexed to pass his credit for him that now he might be safely read; it could not be apprehended less than a disgraceful punishment. Whence to include the whole nation, and those that never yet thus offended, under such a diffident and suspectful prohibition, may plainly be understood what a disparagement it is. So much the more whenas debtors and delinquents may walk abroad without a keeper, but unoffensive books must not stir forth without a visible jailor in their

title.   Nor is it to the common people less than a
reproach ; for if we be so jealous over them as
that we dare not trust them with an English
pamphlet, what do we but censure them for a giddy,
vicious, and ungrounded people ; in such a sick
and weak state of faith and discretion as to be
able to take nothing down but through the pipe of
a licenser?   That this is care or love of them we
cannot pretend, whenas in those popish places,
where the laity are most hated and despised, the
same strictness is used over them.   Wisdom we
cannot call it, because it stops but one breach of
licence, nor that neither : whenas those corruptions
which it seeks to prevent break in faster at other
doors which cannot be shut.

And in conclusion it reflects to the disrepute of
our ministers also, of whose labours we should
hope better, and of their proficiency which their
flock reaps by them, than that after all this light of
the gospel which is, and is to be, and all this
continual preaching, they should be still frequented
with such an unprincipled, unedified, and laic
rabble as that the whiff of every new pamphlet
should stagger them out of their catechism and
Christian walking.   This may have much reason
to discourage the ministers, when such a low
conceit is had of all their exhortations, and the
benefiting of their hearers, as that they are not
thought fit to be turned loose to three sheets of
paper without a licenser ; that all the sermons, all
the lectures preached, printed, vended in such

numbers and such volumes as have now well-nigh made all other books unsaleable, should not be armour enough against one single Enchiridion, without the castle of St. Angelo of an imprimatur.

And lest some should persuade ye, lords and commons, that these arguments of learned men's discouragement at this your order are mere flourishes, and not real, I could recount what I have seen and heard in other countries, where this kind of inquisition tyrannizes; when I have sat among their learned men, (for that honour I had,) and been counted happy to be born in such a place of philosophic freedom, as they supposed England was, while themselves did nothing but bemoan the servile condition into which learning amongst them was brought; that this was it which had damped the glory of Italian wits; that nothing had been there written now these many years but flattery and fustian. There it was that I found and visited the famous Galileo, grown old, a prisoner to the inquisition, for thinking in astronomy otherwise than the Franciscan and Dominican licensers thought. And though I knew that England then was groaning loudest under the prelatical yoke, nevertheless I took it as a pledge of future happiness, that other nations were so persuaded of her liberty.

Yet was it beyond my hope, that those worthies were then breathing in her air who should be her leaders to such a deliverance as shall never be forgotten by any revolution of time that this world hath to finish. When that was once begun, it was

as little in my fear, that what words of complaint
I heard among learned men of other parts uttered
against the inquisition, the same I should hear by
as learned men at home uttered in time of parliament against an order of licensing ; and that so
generally that when I had disclosed myself a
companion of their discontent, I might say, if
without envy, that he whom an honest quæstorship
had endeared to the Sicilians was not more by
them importuned against Verres than the favourable opinion which I had among many who honour
ye, and are known and respected by ye, loaded me
with entreaties and persuasions that I would not
despair to lay together that which just reason
should bring into my mind toward the removal
of an undeserved thraldom upon learning.

That this is not therefore the disburdening of a
particular fancy, but the common grievance of all
those who had prepared their minds and studies
above the vulgar pitch, to advance truth in others,
and from others to entertain it, thus much may
satisfy. And in their name I shall for neither
friend nor foe conceal what the general murmur
is ; that if it come to inquisitioning again, and
licensing, and that we are so timorous of ourselves,
and suspicious of all men, as to fear each book,
and the shaking of each leaf, before we know what
the contents are ; if some who but of late were little
better than silenced from preaching, shall come
now to silence us from reading, except what they
please, it cannot be guessed what is intended by

some but a second tyranny over learning: and will soon put it out of controversy that bishops and presbyters are the same to us, both name and thing.

That those evils of prelaty which before from five or six and twenty sees were distributively charged upon the whole people will now light wholly upon learning, is not obscure to us : whenas now the pastor of a small unlearned parish on the sudden shall be exalted archbishop over a large diocese of books, and yet not remove, but keep his other cure too, a mystical pluralist. He who but of late cried down the sole ordination of every novice bachelor of art, and denied sole jurisdiction over the simplest parishioner, shall now at home in his private chair assume both these over worthiest and excellentest books and ablest authors that write them. This is not the covenants and pro-testations that we have made. This is not to put down prelacy; this is but to chop an episcopacy; this is but to translate the palace metropolitan from one kind of dominion into another; this is but an old canonical sleight of commuting our penance. To startle thus betimes at a mere unlicensed pam-phlet, will, after a while, be afraid of every con-venticle, and a while after will make a conventicle of every Christian meeting.

But I am certain that a state governed by the rules of justice and fortitude, or a church built and founded upon the rock of faith and true knowledge, cannot be so pusillanimous. While things are yet

not constituted in religion, that freedom of writing
should be restrained by a discipline imitated from
the prelates, and learned by them from the inquisition, to shut us up all again into the breast of a
licenser, must needs give cause of doubt and
discouragement to all learned and religious men ;
who cannot but discern the fineness of this politic
drift, and who are the contrivers ; that while
bishops were to be baited down, then all presses
might be open ; it was the people's birthright and
privilege in time of parliament, it was the breaking
forth of light.

But now the bishops abrogated and voided out
of the church, as if our reformation sought no more,
but to make room for others into their seats under
another name ; the episcopal arts begin to bud
again ; the cruse of truth must run no more oil ;
liberty of printing must be enthralled again under
a prelatical commission of twenty ; the privilege
of the people nullified ; and, which is worse, the
freedom of learning must groan again, and to her
old fetters : all this the parliament yet sitting.
Although their own late arguments and defences
against the prelates might remember them that
this obstructing violence meets for the most part
with an event utterly opposite to the end which it
drives at : instead of suppressing sects and schisms
it raises them and invests them with a reputation :
'The punishing of wits enhances their authority,'
saith the Viscount St. Albans; 'and a forbidden
'writing is thought to be a certain spark of truth,

' that flies up in the faces of them who seek to tread
' it out.' This order, therefore, may prove a nursing
mother to sects, but I shall easily shew how it will
be a stepdame to truth : and first, by disenabling
us to the maintenance of what is known already.

Well knows he who uses to consider that our
faith and knowledge thrives by exercise, as well as
our limbs and complexion. Truth is compared in
scripture to a streaming fountain ; if her waters
flow not in a perpetual progression, they sicken
into a muddy pool of conformity and tradition. A
man may be a heretic in the truth ; and if he believe things only because his pastor says so, or the
assembly so determines, without knowing other
reason, though his belief be true, yet the very
truth he holds becomes his heresy. There is not
any burden that some would gladlier post off to
another than the charge and care of their religion.
There be, who knows not that there be ? of protestants and professors who live and die in as
arrant an implicit faith as any lay papist of Loretto.

A wealthy man, addicted to his pleasure and to
his profits, finds religion to be a traffic so entangled, and of so many piddling accounts, that of
all mysteries he cannot skill to keep a stock going
upon that trade. What should he do ? Fain he
would have the name to be religious, fain he would
bear up with his neighbours in that. What does
he therefore, but resolves to give over toiling, and
to find himself out some factor, to whose care and
credit he may commit the whole managing of his

religious affairs ; some divine of note and estimation that must be. To him he adheres, resigns
the whole warehouse of his religion, with all the
locks and keys, into his custody; and indeed
makes the very person of that man his religion ;
esteems his associating with him a sufficient evidence and commendatory of his own piety. So
that a man may say his religion is now no more
within himself, but is become a dividual movable,
and goes and comes near him according as that
good man frequents the house. He entertains
him, gives him gifts, feasts him, lodges him ; his
religion comes home at night, prays, is liberally
supped, and sumptuously laid to sleep ; rises, is
saluted, and after the malmsey, or some well-
spiced bruage, and better breakfasted than He
whose morning appetite would have gladly fed on
green figs between Bethany and Jerusalem, his
religion walks abroad at eight, and leaves his kind
entertainer in the shop trading all day without his
religion.

Another sort there be who when they hear that
all things shall be ordered, all things regulated and
settled, nothing written but what passes through
the custom-house of certain publicans that have the
tonnaging and poundaging of all free-spoken truth,
will straight give themselves up into your hands,
make them and cut them out what religion ye
please : there be delights, there be recreations and
jolly pastimes, that will fetch the day about from
sun to sun, and rock the tedious year as in a

delightful dream. What need they torture their
heads with that which others have taken so strictly
and so unalterably into their own purveying?
These are the fruits which a dull ease and cessa-
tion of our knowledge will bring forth among the
people. How goodly and how to be wished were
such an obedient unanimity as this ! What a fine
conformity would it starch us all into ! Doubtless
a staunch and solid piece of framework as any
January could freeze together.

Nor much better will be the consequence even
among the clergy themselves: it is no new thing
never heard of before for a parochial minister,
who has his reward and is at his Hercules' pillars
in a warm benefice, to be easily inclinable, if he
have nothing else that may rouse up his studies,
to finish his circuit in an English Concordance and
a topic folio, the gatherings and savings of a sober
graduateship, a Harmony and a Catena, treading
the constant round of certain common doctrinal
heads, attended with their uses, motives, marks,
and means ; out of which, as out of an alphabet or
sol-fa, by forming and transforming, joining and
disjoining variously, a little bookcraft and two
hours' meditation might furnish him unspeakably
to the performance of more than a weekly charge
of sermoning : not to reckon up the infinite helps
of interlinearies, breviaries, synopses, and other
loitering gear. But as for the multitude of sermons
ready printed and piled up, on every text that is
not difficult, our London trading St. Thomas in

his vestry, and add to boot St. Martin and St. Hugh, have not within their hallowed limits more vendible ware of all sorts ready made: so that penury he never need fear of pulpit provision, having where so plenteously to refresh his magazine. But if his rear and flanks be not impaled, if his back door be not secured by the rigid licenser, but that a bold book may now and then issue forth and give the assault to some of his old collections in their trenches, it will concern him then to keep waking, to stand in watch, to set good guards and sentinels about his received opinions, to walk the round and counter-round with his fellow-inspectors, fearing lest any of his flock be seduced, who also then would be better instructed, better exercised and disciplined. And God fend that the fear of this diligence, which must then be used, do not make us affect the laziness of a licensing church?

For if we be sure we are in the right, and do not hold the truth guiltily, which becomes not, if we ourselves condemn not our own weak and frivolous teaching, and the people for an untaught and irreligious gadding rout; what can be more fair than when a man judicious, learned, and of a conscience, for aught we know, as good as theirs that taught us what we know, shall not privily from house to house, which is more dangerous, but openly by writing, publish to the world what his opinion is, what his reasons, and wherefore that which is now thought cannot be sound? Christ urged it as wherewith to justify himself, that he preached in public; yet writing is more public than preaching, and more easy to refutation if need be, there being so many whose business and profession merely it is to be the champions of truth; which if they neglect, what can be imputed but their sloth or inability?

Thus much we are hindered and disinured by this course of licensing toward the true knowledge of what we seem to know. For how much it hurts and hinders the licensers themselves in the calling of their ministry, more than any secular employment, if they will discharge that office as they ought, so that of necessity they must neglect either the one duty or the other, I insist not, because it is a particular, but leave it to their own conscience, how they will decide it there.

There is yet behind of what I purposed to lay open, the incredible loss and detriment that this plot of licensing puts us to. More than if some enemy at sea should stop up all our havens, and ports, and creeks, it hinders and retards the importation of our richest merchandise,—truth: nay, it was first established and put in practice by antichristian malice and mystery, on set purpose to extinguish, if it were possible, the light of reformation, and to settle falsehood; little differing from that policy wherewith the Turk upholds his Alcoran, by the prohibiting of printing. It is not denied, but gladly confessed, we are to send our thanks and vows to heaven louder than most of nations for that great measure of truth which we enjoy, especially in those main points between us and the pope, with his appurtenances the prelates: but he who thinks we are to pitch our tent here, and have attained the utmost prospect of reformation that the mortal glass wherein we contemplate can shew us, till we come to beatific vision, that man by this very opinion declares that he is yet far short of truth.

Truth indeed came once into the world with her divine Master, and was a perfect shape most glorious to look on : but when he ascended, and his apostles after him were laid asleep, then straight arose a wicked race of deceivers, who, as that story goes of the Egyptian Typhon with his conspirators, how they dealt with the good Osiris, took the virgin Truth, hewed her lovely form into a thousand pieces, and scattered them to the four winds. From that time ever since, the sad friends of Truth, such as durst appear, imitating the careful search that Isis made for the mangled body of Osiris, went up and down gathering up limb by limb still as they could find them. We have not yet found them all, lords and commons, nor ever shall do, till her Master's second coming ; he shall bring together every joint and member, and shall mould them into an immortal feature of loveliness and perfection. Suffer not these licensing prohibitions to stand at every place of opportunity forbidding and disturbing them that continue seeking, that

continue to do our obsequies to the torn body of
our martyred saint.

We boast our light; but if we look not wisely
on the sun itself, it smites us into darkness. Who
can discern those planets that are oft combust, and
those stars of brightest magnitude that rise and set
with the sun, until the opposite motion of their
orbs bring them to such a place in the firmament,
where they may be seen evening or morning? The
light which we have gained was given us, not to
be ever staring on, but by it to discover onward
things more remote from our knowledge. It is not
the unfrocking of a priest, the unmitring of a
bishop, and the removing him from off the presbyterian shoulders, that will make us a happy nation :
no ; if other things as great in the church, and in
the rule of life both economical and political, be
not looked into and reformed, we have looked so
long upon the blaze that Zuinglius and Calvin
have beaconed up to us, that we are stark blind.

There be who perpetually complain of schisms
and sects, and make it such a calamity that any
man dissents from their maxims. It is their own
pride and ignorance which causes the disturbing,
who neither will hear with meekness, nor can convince, yet all must be suppressed which is not
found in their Syntagma. They are the troublers,
they are the dividers of unity, who neglect and
permit not others to unite those dissevered pieces
which are yet wanting to the body of Truth. To be
still searching what we know not by what we

12

know, still closing up truth to truth as we find it, (for all her body is homogeneal, and proportional,) this is the golden rule in theology as well as in arithmetic, and makes up the best harmony in a church ; not the forced and outward union of cold and neutral and inwardly divided minds.

Lords and commons of England, consider what nation it is whereof ye are, and whereof ye are the governors : a nation not slow and dull, but of a quick, ingenious, and piercing spirit, acute to invent, subtile and sinewy to discourse, not beneath the reach of any point the highest that human capacity can soar to. Therefore the studies of learning in her deepest sciences have been so ancient and so eminent among us, that writers of good antiquity and able judgment have been persuaded that even the school of Pythagoras, and the Persian wisdom, took beginning from the old philosophy of this island. And that wise and civil Roman, Julius Agricola, who governed once here for Cæsar, preferred the natural wits of Britain before the laboured studies of the French. Nor is it for nothing that the grave and frugal Transylvanian sends out yearly from as far as the mountainous borders of Russia, and beyond the Hercynian wilderness, not their youth, but their staid men, to learn our language and our theologic arts. Yet that which is above all this, the favour and the love of Heaven, we have great argument to think in a peculiar manner propitious and propending toward us. Why else was this nation chosen before any other, that out of her, as out of Sion, should be proclaimed and sounded forth the first tidings and trumpet of reformation to all Europe? And had it not been the obstinate perverseness of our prelates against the divine and admirable spirit of Wicklef, to suppress him as a schismatic and innovator, perhaps neither the Bohemian Husse and Jerome, no, nor the name of Luther or of Calvin, had been ever known : the glory of reforming all our neighbours had been completely ours. But now, as our obdurate clergy have with violence demeaned the matter, we are become hitherto the latest and the backwardest scholars of whom God offered to have made us the teachers.

Now once again by all concurrence of signs, and by the general instinct of holy and devout men, as they daily and solemnly express their thoughts, God is decreeing to begin some new and great period in his church, even to the reforming of reformation itself; what does he then but reveal himself to his servants, and as his manner is, first to his Englishmen? I say, as his manner is, first to us, though we mark not the method of his counsels, and are unworthy. Behold now this vast city, a city of refuge, the mansion-house of liberty, encompassed and surrounded with his protection ; the shop of war hath not there more anvils and hammers working, to fashion out the plates and instruments of armed justice in defence of beleaguered truth, than there be pens and heads there, sitting by their studious lamps, musing, searching, revolving new notions and ideas wherewith to present, as with their homage and their fealty, the approaching reformation: others as fast reading, trying all things, assenting to the force of reason and convincement.

What could a man require more from a nation so pliant and so prone to seek after knowledge? What wants there to such a towardly and pregnant soil but wise and faithful labourers to make a knowing people, a nation of prophets, of sages, and of worthies? We reckon more than five months yet to harvest; there need not be five weeks; had we but eyes to lift up, the fields are white already. Where there is much desire to learn, there of necessity will be much arguing, much writing, many opinions; for opinion in good men is but knowledge in the making. Under these fantastic terrors of sect and schism we wrong the earnest and zealous thirst after knowledge and understanding which God hath stirred up in this city. What some lament of, we rather should rejoice at, should rather praise this pious forwardness among men to reassume the ill-deputed care of their religion into their own hands again. A little generous prudence, a little forbearance of one another, and some grain of charity might win all these diligences to join and unite into one general and brotherly search after truth; could we but forego this prelatical tradition of crowding free consciences and Christian liberties into canons and precepts of men. I doubt not, if some great and worthy stranger should come among us, wise to discern the mould and temper of a people, and how to govern it, observing the high hopes and aims, the diligent alacrity of our extended thoughts and reasonings in the pursuance of truth and freedom, but that he would cry out as Pyrrhus did, admiring the Roman docility and courage, ' If ' such were my Epirots, I would not despair the ' greatest design that could be attempted to make ' a church or kingdom happy.'

Yet these are the men cried out against for schismatics and sectaries, as if, while the temple of the Lord was building, some cutting, some squaring the marble, others hewing the cedars, there should be a sort of irrational men who could not consider there must be many schisms and many dissections made in the quarry and in the timber ere the house of God can be built. And when every stone is laid artfully together, it cannot be united into a continuity, it can but be contiguous in this world : neither can every piece of the building be of one form ; nay, rather the perfection consists in this, that out of many moderate varieties and brotherly dissimilitudes that are not vastly disproportional arises the goodly and the graceful symmetry that commends the whole pile and structure.

Let us therefore be more considerate builders, more wise in spiritual architecture, when great reformation is expected. For now the time seems come, wherein Moses, the great prophet, may sit

in heaven rejoicing to see that memorable and
glorious wish of his fulfilled, when not only our
seventy elders but all the Lord's people are become
prophets. No marvel then though some men, and
some good men too perhaps, but young in goodness,
as Joshua then was, envy them. They fret, and
out of their own weakness are in agony, lest these
divisions and subdivisions will undo us. The
adversary again applauds, and waits the hour :
when they have branched themselves out, saith
he, small enough into parties and partitions, then
will be our time. Fool ! he sees not the firm root,
out of which we all grow, though into branches ;
nor will beware, until he see our small divided
maniples cutting through at every angle of his ill-
united and unwieldy brigade. And that we are to
hope better of all these supposed sects and schisms,
and that we shall not need that solicitude, honest
perhaps, though overtimorous, of them that vex in
this behalf, but shall laugh in the end at those
malicious applauders of our differences, I have these
reasons to persuade me.

First, when a city shall be as it were besieged
and blocked about, her navigable river infested,
inroads and incursions round, defiance and battle
oft rumoured to be marching up even to her walls
and suburb trenches ; that then the people, or the
greater part, more than at other times, wholly
taken up with the study of highest and most important matters to be reformed, should be disputing,
reasoning, reading, inventing, discoursing, even to

a rarity and admiration, things not before discoursed or written of, argues first a singular good
will, contentedness, and confidence in your prudent
foresight, and safe government, lords and commons; and from thence derives itself to a gallant
bravery and well-grounded contempt of their enemies, as if there were no small number of as great
spirits among us as his was who, when Rome was
nigh besieged by Hannibal, being in the city,
bought that piece of ground at no cheap rate
whereon Hannibal himself encamped his own
regiment.

Next, it is a lively and cheerful presage of our
happy success and victory. For as in a body when
the blood is fresh, the spirits pure and vigorous,
not only to vital but to rational faculties, and those
in the acutest and the pertest operations of wit and
subtlety, it argues in what good plight and constitution the body is ; so when the cheerfulness of the
people is so sprightly up, as that it has not only
wherewith to guard well its own freedom and
safety, but to spare, and to bestow upon the
solidest and sublimest points of controversy and new
invention, it betokens us not degenerated, nor
drooping to a fatal decay, but casting off the old
and wrinkled skin of corruption to outlive these
pangs, and wax young again, entering the glorious
ways of truth and prosperous virtue, destined to
become great and honourable in these latter ages.
Methinks I see in my mind a noble and puissant
nation rousing herself like a strong man after sleep,

and shaking her invincible locks. Methinks I see her as an eagle mewing her mighty youth, and kindling her undazzled eyes at the full midday beam, purging and unscaling her long-abused sight at the fountain itself of heavenly radiance; while the whole noise of timorous and flocking birds, with those also that love the twilight, flutter about, amazed at what she means, and in their envious gabble would prognosticate a year of sects and schisms.

What should ye do then, should ye suppress all this flowery crop of knowledge and new light sprung up and yet springing daily in this city, should ye set an oligarchy of twenty engrossers over it, to bring a famine upon our minds again, when we shall know nothing but what is measured to us by their bushel? Believe it, lords and commons, they who counsel ye to such a suppressing do as good as bid ye suppress yourselves; and I will soon show how. If it be desired to know the immediate cause of all this free writing and free speaking, there cannot be assigned a truer than your own mild and free and humane government; it is the liberty, lords and commons, which your own valorous and happy counsels have purchased us; liberty which is the nurse of all great wits; this is that which hath rarified and enlightened our spirits like the influence of heaven; this is that which hath enfranchised, enlarged, and lifted up our apprehensions degrees above themselves. Ye cannot make us now less capable, less knowing, less eagerly pursuing of the truth, unless ye first make yourselves, that made us so, less the lovers, less the founders of our true liberty. We can grow ignorant again, brutish, formal, and slavish, as ye found us ; but you then must first become that which ye cannot be, oppressive, arbitrary, and tyrannous, as they were from whom ye have freed us. That our hearts are now more capacious, our thoughts more erected to the search and expectation of greatest and exactest things, is the issue of your own virtue propagated in us ; ye cannot suppress that, unless ye reinforce an abrogated and merciless law, that fathers may dispatch at will their own children. And who shall then stick closest to ye and excite others? Not he who takes up arms for coat and conduct,[1] and his four nobles of Danegelt. Although I dispraise not the defence of just immunities, yet love my peace better, if that were all. Give me the liberty to know, to utter, and to argue freely according to conscience, above all liberties.

What would be best advised then, if it be found so hurtful and so unequal to suppress opinions for the newness or the unsuitableness to a customary acceptance, will not be my task to say ; I shall only repeat what I have learned from one of your own honourable number, a right noble and pious lord, who had he not sacrificed his life and fortunes to the church and commonwealth, we had not now missed and bewailed a worthy and undoubted patron of this argument. Ye know him, I am sure ; yet I for honour's sake, and may it be eternal

[1] Taxation for the clothing and conveyance of troops.—ED.

to him, shall name him, the Lord Brook. He writing of episcopacy, and by the way treating of sects and schisms, left ye his vote, or rather now the last words of his dying charge, which I know will ever be of dear and honoured regard with ye, so full of meekness and breathing charity, that next to His last testament, who bequeathed love and peace to his disciples, I cannot call to mind where I have read or heard words more mild and peaceful. He there exhorts us to hear with patience and humility those, however they be miscalled, that desire to live purely in such a use of God's ordinances as the best guidance of their conscience gives them, and to tolerate them, though in some disconformity to ourselves. The book itself will tell us more at large, being published to the world and dedicated to the parliament by him who both for his life and for his death deserves that what advice he left be not laid by without perusal.

And now the time in special is, by privilege to write and speak what may help to the further discussing of matters in agitation. The temple of Janus, with his two controversial faces, might now not unsignificantly be set open. And though all the winds of doctrine were let loose to play upon the earth, so Truth be in the field, we do injuriously by licensing and prohibiting to misdoubt her strength. Let her and Falsehood grapple; who ever knew Truth put to the worse, in a free and open encounter? Her confuting is the best and surest suppressing. He who hears what praying there is for light and clear knowledge to be sent down among us, would think of other matters to be constituted beyond the discipline of Geneva, framed and fabricated already to our hands.

Yet when the new light which we beg for shines in upon us, there be who envy and oppose, if it come not first in at their casements. What a collusion is this, whenas we are exhorted by the wise man to use diligence, 'to seek for wisdom as for 'hidden treasures,' early and late, that another order shall enjoin us to know nothing but by statute? When a man hath been labouring the hardest labour in the deep mines of knowledge, hath furnished out his findings in all their equipage, drawn forth his reasons as it were a battle ranged, scattered and defeated all objections in his way, calls out his adversary into the plain, offers him the advantage of wind and sun, if he please, only that he may try the matter by dint of argument ; for his opponents then to skulk, to lay ambushments, to keep a narrow bridge of licensing where the challenger should pass, though it be valour enough in soldiership, is but weakness and cowardice in the wars of truth. For who knows not that Truth is strong, next to the Almighty ; she needs no policies, nor stratagems, nor licensings to make her victorious ; those are the shifts and the defences that error uses against her power ; give her but room, and do not bind her when she sleeps, for then she speaks not true, as the old Proteus did,

who spoke oracles only when he was caught and
bound, but then rather she turns herself into all
shapes except her own, and perhaps tunes her voice
according to the time, as Micaiah did before Ahab,
until she be adjured into her own likeness.

Yet is it not impossible that she may have more
shapes than one. What else is all that rank of
things indifferent, wherein truth may be on this
side or on the other without being unlike herself?
What but a vain shadow else is the abolition of
' those ordinances, that hand-writing nailed to the
' cross,' what great purchase is this Christian
liberty which Paul so often boasts of? His doctrine
is, that he who eats or eats not, regards a day or
regards it not, may do either to the Lord. How
many other things might be tolerated in peace, and
left to conscience, had we but charity, and were it
not the chief stronghold of our hypocrisy to be ever
judging one another? I fear yet this iron yoke of
outward conformity hath left a slavish print upon our
necks ; the ghost of a linen decency yet haunts us.
We stumble, and are impatient at the least dividing
of one visible congregation from another, though it
be not in fundamentals ; and through our forwardness to suppress, and our backwardness to recover
any enthralled piece of truth out of the gripe of
custom, we care not to keep truth separated from
truth, which is the fiercest rent and disunion of all.
We do not see that while we still affect by all
means a rigid external formality, we may as soon
fall again into a gross conforming stupidity, a stark

and dead congealment of 'wood and hay and 'stubble' forced and frozen together, which is more to the sudden degenerating of a church than many subdichotomies of petty schisms.

Not that I can think well of every light separation ; or that all in a church is to be expected 'gold and silver and precious stones :' it is not possible for man to sever the wheat from the tares, the good fish from the other fry ; that must be the angels' ministry at the end of mortal things. Yet if all cannot be of one mind, as who looks they should be? this doubtless is more wholesome, more prudent, and more Christian, that many be tolerated rather than all compelled. I mean not tolerated popery, and open superstition, which as it extirpates all religions and civil supremacies, so itself should be extirpate, provided first that all charitable and compassionate means be used to win and regain the weak and the misled : that also which is impious or evil absolutely either against faith or manners no law can possibly permit that intends not to unlaw itself : but those neighbouring differences, or rather indifferences, are what I speak of, whether in some point of doctrine or of discipline, which though they may be many, yet need not interrupt the unity of spirit, if we could but find among us the bond of peace.

In the meanwhile, if any one would write, and bring his helpful hand to the slow-moving reformation which we labour under, if truth have spoken to him before others, or but seemed at least to

speak, who hath so bejesuited us that we should
trouble that man with asking licence to do so
worthy a deed? and not consider this, that if it
come to prohibiting, there is not aught more likely
to be prohibited than truth itself: whose first
appearance to our eyes, bleared and dimmed with
prejudice and custom, is more unsightly and un-
plausible than many errors; even as the person is
of many a great man slight and contemptible to see
to.   And what do they tell us vainly of new
opinions, when this very opinion of theirs, that none
must be heard but whom they like, is the worst and
newest opinion of all others; and is the chief cause
why sects and schisms do so much abound, and true
knowledge is kept at distance from us? Besides yet
a greater danger which is in it: for when God
shakes a kingdom with strong and healthful commotions to a general reforming, it is not untrue
that many sectaries and false teachers are then
busiest in seducing; but yet more true it is that
God then raises to his own work men of rare
abilities and more than common industry, not
only to look back and revive what hath been
taught heretofore, but to gain further, and to
go on some new enlightened steps in the discovery of truth.   For such is the order of God's
enlightening his church, to dispense and deal
out by degrees his beam, so as our earthly eyes
may best sustain it.   Neither is God appointed and
confined, where and out of what place these his
chosen shall be first heard to speak; for he sees

not as man sees, chooses not as man chooses, lest
we should devote ourselves again to set places and
assemblies, and outward callings of men ; planting
our faith one while in the old convocation house,
and another while in the chapel at Westminster ;
when all the faith and religion that shall be there
canonized is not sufficient without plain convincement, and the charity of patient instruction, to
supple the least bruise of conscience, to edify the
meanest Christian who desires to walk in the
spirit, and not in the letter of human trust, for all
the number of voices that can be there made ; no,
though Harry the Seventh himself there, with all
his liege tombs about him, should lend them voices
from the dead to swell their number.

And if the men be erroneous who appear to be
the leading schismatics, what withholds us but our
sloth, our self-will, and distrust in the right cause,
that we do not give them gentle meetings and
gentle dismissions, that we debate not and examine
the matter thoroughly with liberal and frequent
audience ; if not for their sakes yet for our own ?
Seeing no man who hath tasted learning, but will
confess the many ways of profiting by those who,
not contented with stale receipts, are able to
manage and set forth new positions to the world.
And were they but as the dust and cinders of our
feet, so long as in that notion they may yet serve
to polish and brighten the armoury of truth, even
for that respect they were not utterly to be cast
away. But if they be of those whom God hath

fitted for the special use of these times with eminent and ample gifts, and those perhaps neither among the priests nor among the pharisees, and we, in the haste of a precipitant zeal, shall make no distinction, but resolve to stop their mouths, because we fear they come with new and dangerous opinions, as we commonly forejudge them ere we understand them ; no less than woe to us, while, thinking thus to defend the gospel, we are found the persecutors !

There have been not a few since the beginning of this parliament, both of the presbytery and others, who by their unlicensed books to the contempt of an imprimatur first broke that triple ice clung about our hearts, and taught the people to see day; I hope that none of those were the persuaders to renew upon us this bondage which they themselves have wrought so much good by contemning. But if neither the check that Moses gave to young Joshua, nor the countermand which our Saviour gave to young John, who was so ready to prohibit those whom he thought unlicensed, be not enough to admonish our elders how unacceptable to God their testy mood of prohibiting is; if neither their own remembrance what evil hath abounded in the church by this lett of licensing, and what good they themselves have begun by transgressing it, be not enough, but that they will persuade and execute the most Dominican part of the inquisition over us, and are already with one foot in the stirrup so active at suppressing, it would be no unequal distribution in the first place to suppress the suppressors themselves; whom the change of their condition hath puffed up, more than their late experience of harder times hath made wise.

And as for regulating the press, let no man think to have the honour of advising ye better than yourselves have done in that order published next before this, 'That no book be printed, unless the printer's 'and the author's name, or at least the printer's be 'registered.' Those which otherwise come forth, if they be found mischievous and libellous, the fire and the executioner will be the timeliest and the most effectual remedy that man's prevention can use. For this authentic Spanish policy of licensing books, if I have said aught, will prove the most unlicensed book itself within a short while; and was the immediate image of a star-chamber decree to that purpose made in those times when that court did the rest of those her pious works, for which she is now fallen from the stars with Lucifer. Whereby ye may guess what kind of state prudence, what love of the people, what care of religion or good manners there was at the contriving, although with singular hypocrisy it pretended to bind books to their good behaviour. And how it got the upper hand of your precedent order so well constituted before, if we may believe those men whose profession gives them cause to inquire most, it may be doubted there was in it the fraud of some old patentees and monopolizers in the trade of book-selling; who, under pretence of the poor in their company not to be defrauded, and the just retaining

13

of each man his several copy, (which God forbid
should be gainsaid,) brought divers glossing colours
to the House, which were indeed but colours, and
serving to no end except it be to exercise a superiority over their neighbours; men who do not
therefore labour in an honest profession, to which
learning is indebted, that they should be made
other men's vassals.   Another end is thought was
aimed at by some of them in procuring by petition
this order, that having power in their hands, malignant books might the easier escape abroad, as the
event shews.   But of these sophisms and elenchs
of merchandise I skill not : this I know, that errors
in a good government and in a bad are equally
almost incident ; for what magistrate may not be
misinformed, and much the sooner, if liberty of
printing be reduced into the power of a few?   But
to redress willingly and speedily what hath been
erred, and in highest authority to esteem a plain
advertisement more than others have done a
sumptuous bribe, is a virtue, honoured lords and
commons, answerable to your highest actions, and
whereof none can participate but greatest and
wisest men.

THE TENURE OF KINGS AND MAGISTRATES

PROVING THAT IT IS LAWFUL, AND HATH BEEN HELD SO THROUGH ALL AGES, FOR ANY WHO HAVE THE POWER TO CALL TO ACCOUNT A TYRANT OR WICKED KING, AND AFTER DUE CONVICTION TO DEPOSE AND PUT HIM TO DEATH, IF THE ORDINARY MAGISTRATE HAVE NEGLECTED OR DENIED TO DO IT: AND THAT THEY WHO OF LATE SO MUCH BLAME DEPOSING ARE THE MEN THAT DID IT THEMSELVES. 1649.

THE TENURE OF KINGS AND MAGISTRATES.

IF men within themselves would be governed by reason, and not generally give up their understanding to a double tyranny, of custom from without and blind affections within, they would discern better what it is to favour and uphold the tyrant of a nation. But, being slaves within doors, no wonder that they strive so much to have the public state conformably governed to the inward vicious rule by which they govern themselves. For indeed none can love freedom heartily but good men ; the rest love not freedom but licence, which never hath more scope or more indulgence than under tyrants. Hence is it that tyrants are not oft offended nor stand much in doubt of bad men, as being all naturally servile ; but in whom virtue and true worth most is eminent, them they fear in earnest, as by right their masters ; against them lies all their hatred and suspicion. Consequently, neither do bad men hate tyrants, but have been always readiest, with the falsified names of loyalty and obedience, to colour over their base compliances.

And although sometimes for shame, and when it comes to their own grievances, of purse especially, they would seem good patriots, and side with the better cause, yet when others for the deliverance of their country endued with fortitude and heroic virtue to fear nothing but the curse written against those ' that do the work of the Lord negligently ' would go on to remove, not only the calamities and thraldoms of a people, but the roots and causes whence they spring ; straight these men, and sure helpers at need, as if they hated only the miseries but not the mischiefs, after they have juggled and paltered with the world, bandied and borne arms against their king, divested him, disanointed him, nay, cursed him all over in their pulpits and their pamphlets, to the engaging of sincere and real men beyond what is possible or honest to retreat from, not only turn revolters from those principles which only could at first move them, but lay the strain of disloyalty, and worse, on those proceedings which are the necessary consequences of their own former actions ; nor disliked by themselves, were they managed to the entire advantages of their own faction ; not considering the while that he toward whom they boasted their new fidelity, counted them accessory, and by those statutes and laws which they so impotently brandish against others would have doomed them to a traitor's death for what they have done already.

It is true that most men are apt enough to civil

wars and commotions as a novelty, and for a flash
hot and active ; but through sloth or inconstancy,
and weakness of spirit, either fainting ere their
own pretences, though never so just, be half
attained, or through an inbred falsehood and
wickedness betray ofttimes to destruction with
themselves men of noblest temper joined with them
for causes whereof they in their rash undertakings
were not capable. If God and a good cause give
them victory, the prosecution whereof for the most
part inevitably draws after it the alteration of laws,
change of government, downfall of princes with
their families ; then comes the task to those
worthies which are the soul of that enterprise, to
be sweat and laboured out amidst the throng and
noses of vulgar and irrational men. Some contest-
ing for privileges, customs, forms, and that old
entanglement of iniquity, their gibberish laws,
though the badge of their ancient slavery. Others,
who have been fiercest against their prince under
the notion of a tyrant, and no mean incendiaries of
the war against him, when God, out of his providence and high disposal hath delivered him into the
hand of their brethren, on a sudden and in a new
garb of allegiance, which their doings have long
since cancelled, they plead for him, pity him, extol
him, protest against those that talk of bringing
him to the trial of justice, which is the sword of
God, superior to all mortal things, in whose hand
soever by apparent signs his testified will is to
put it.

But certainly, if we consider who and what they are, on a sudden grown so pitiful, we may conclude their pity can be no true and Christian commiseration, but either levity and shallowness of mind, or else a carnal admiring of that worldly pomp and greatness from whence they see him fallen ; or rather, lastly, a dissembled and seditious pity, feigned of industry to beget new discord. As for mercy, if it be to a tyrant, under which name they themselves have cited him so oft in the hearing of God, of angels, and the holy church assembled, and there charged him with the spilling of more innocent blood by far than ever Nero did, undoubtedly the mercy which they pretend is the mercy of wicked men : and 'their mercies,' we read, 'are cruelties;' hazarding the welfare of a whole nation, to have saved one whom they so oft have termed Agag, and vilifying the blood of many Jonathans who have saved Israel ; insisting with much niceness on the unnecessariest clause of their covenant wrested, wherein the fear of change and the absurd contradiction of a flattering hostility had hampered them, but not scrupling to give away for compliments, to an implacable revenge, the heads of many thousand Christians more.

Another sort there is, who coming in the course of these affairs to have their share in great actions above the form of law or custom, at least to give their voice and approbation, begin to swerve and almost shiver at the majesty and grandeur of some noble deed, as if they were newly entered into a great sin; disputing precedents, forms, and circumstances, when the commonwealth nigh perishes for want of deeds in substance, done with just and faithful expedition. To these I wish better instruction, and virtue equal to their calling; the former of which, that is to say, instruction, I shall endeavour, as my duty is, to bestow on them; and exhort them not to startle from the just and pious resolution of adhering with all their strength and assistance to the present parliament and army, in the glorious way wherein justice and victory hath set them—the only warrants through all ages, next under immediate revelation, to exercise supreme power—in those proceedings, which hitherto appear equal to what hath been done in any age or nation heretofore justly or magnanimously.

Nor let them be discouraged or deterred by any new apostate scarecrows, who, under shew of giving counsel, send out their barking monitories and mementoes, empty of aught else but the spleen of a frustrated faction. For how can that pretended counsel be either sound or faithful, when they that give it see not, for madness and vexation of their ends lost, that those statutes and scriptures which both falsely and scandalously they wrest against their friends and associates, would, by sentence of the common adversary, fall first and heaviest upon their own heads? Neither by mild and tender dispositions be foolishly softened from their duty and perseverance with the unmasculine rhetoric of any puling priest or chaplain, sent as a friendly letter of advice, for fashion's sake in private, and forthwith published by the sender himself, that we may know how much of friend there was in it, to cast an odious envy upon them to whom it was pretended to be sent in charity. Nor let any man be deluded by either the ignorance or the notorious hypocrisy and self-repugnance of our dancing divines, who have the conscience and the boldness to come with scripture in their mouths, glossed and fitted for their turns with a double contradictory sense, transforming the sacred verity of God to an idol with two faces, looking at once two several ways; and with the same quotations to charge others which in the same case they made serve to justify themselves. For while the hope to be made classic and provincial lords led them on, while pluralities greased them thick and deep, to the shame and scandal of religion, more than all the sects and heresies they exclaim against; then to fight against the king's person, and no less a party of his lords and commons, or to put force upon both the Houses, was good, was lawful, was no resisting of superior powers; they only were powers not to be resisted who countenanced the good and punished the evil.

But now that their censorious domineering is not suffered to be universal, truth and conscience to be freed, tithes and pluralities to be no more, though competent allowance provided, and the warm experience of large gifts, and they so good at taking them; yet now to exclude and seize upon impeached members, to bring delinquents without exemption to a fair tribunal by the common national law against murder, is now to be no less than Korah, Dathan, and Abiram. He who but erewhile in the pulpits was a cursed tyrant, an enemy to God and saints, laden with all the innocent blood spilt in three kingdoms, and so to be fought against; is now, though nothing penitent or altered from his first principles, a lawful magistrate, a sovereign lord, the Lord's anointed, not to be touched, though by themselves imprisoned. As if this only were obedience, to preserve the mere useless bulk of his person, and that only in prison, not in the field, not to disobey his commands, deny him his dignity and office, everywhere to resist his power, but where they think it only surviving in their own faction.

But who in particular is a tyrant, cannot be determined in a general discourse otherwise than by supposition; his particular charge, and the sufficient proof of it, must determine that: which I leave to magistrates, at least to the uprighter sort of them, and of the people, though in number less by many, in whom faction least hath prevailed above the law of nature and right reason, to judge as they find cause. But this I dare own as part of my faith, that if such a one there be, by whose commission whole massacres have been committed on his faithful subjects, his provinces offered to pawn or alienation, as the hire of those whom he had solicited to come in and destroy whole cities and countries; be he king, or tyrant, or emperor, the sword of justice is above him; in whose hand soever is found sufficient power to avenge the effusion, and so great a deluge of innocent blood. For if all human power to execute, not accidentally but intendedly, the wrath of God upon evil-doers without exception, be of God; then that power, whether ordinary, or if that fail, extraordinary, so executing that intent of God, is lawful, and not to be resisted. But to unfold more at large this whole question, though with all expedient brevity, I shall here set down, from first beginning, the original of kings; how and wherefore exalted to that dignity above their brethren; and from thence shall prove, that turning to tyranny they may be as lawfully deposed and punished as they were first elected: this I shall do by authorities and reasons, not learnt in corners among schisms and heresies, as our doubling divines are ready to calumniate, but fetched out of the midst of choicest and most authentic learning, and no prohibited authors, nor many heathen, but Mosaical, Christian, orthodoxal, and, which must needs be more convincing to our adversaries, presbyterial.

No man who knows aught can be so stupid to deny that all men naturally were born free, being the image and resemblance of God himself, and were, by privilege above all the creatures, born to command and not to obey: and that they lived so, till from the root of Adam's transgression falling among themselves to do wrong and violence, and foreseeing that such courses must needs tend to the destruction of them all, they agreed by common league to bind each other from mutual injury, and jointly to defend themselves against any that gave disturbance or opposition to such agreement. Hence came cities, towns, and commonwealths. And because no faith in all was found sufficiently binding, they saw it needful to ordain some authority that might restrain by force and punishment what was violated against peace and common right.

This authority and power of self-defence and preservation being originally and naturally in every one of them, and unitedly in them all; for ease, for order, and lest each man should be his own partial judge, they communicated and derived either to one, whom for the eminence of his wisdom and integrity they chose above the rest, or to more than one, whom they thought of equal deserving: the first was called a king; the other, magistrates: not to be their lords and masters, (though afterward those names in some places were given voluntarily to such as had been authors of inestimable good to the people,) but to be their deputies and commissioners, to execute, by virtue of their intrusted power, that justice which else every man by the bond of nature and of covenant must have executed for himself and for one another. And to him that shall consider well why among free persons one man by civil right should bear authority and jurisdiction over another, no other end or reason can be imaginable.

These for a time governed well, and with much equity decided all things at their own arbitrament; till the temptation of such a power, left absolute in their hands, perverted them at length to injustice and partiality. Then did they, who now by trial had found the danger and inconveniencies of committing arbitrary power to any, invent laws, either framed or consented to by all, that should confine and limit the authority of whom they chose to govern them: that so man, of whose failing they had proof, might no more rule over them, but law and reason, abstracted as much as might be from personal errors and frailties. 'While, as the magistrate was set above the ' people, so the law was set above the magistrate.' When this would not serve, but that the law was either not executed, or misapplied, they were constrained from that time, the only remedy left them, to put conditions and take oaths from all kings and magistrates at their first instalment, to do impartial justice by law: who upon those terms and no other received allegiance from the people, that is to say, bond or covenant to obey them in execution of those laws, which they, the people, had themselves made or assented to. And this ofttimes with express warning, that if the king or magistrate proved unfaithful to his trust, the people would be disengaged. They added also counsellors and parliaments, not to be only at his beck, but, with him or without him, at set times, or at all times when any danger threatened, to have care of the public safety. Therefore saith Claudius Sesell, a French statesman, 'The parliament was 'set as a bridle to the king;' which I instance rather, not because our English lawyers have not said the same long before, but because that French monarchy is granted by all to be a far more absolute one than ours. That this and the rest of what hath hitherto been spoken is most true, might be copiously made appear through all stories, heathen and Christian; even of those nations where kings and emperors have sought means to abolish all ancient memory of the people's right by their encroachments and usurpations. But I spare long insertions, appealing to the German, French, Italian, Arragonian, English, and not least the Scottish histories: not forgetting this only by the way, that William the Norman, though a conqueror, and not unsworn at his coronation, was compelled a second time to take oath at St. Alban's ere the people would be brought to yield obedience.

It being thus manifest that the power of kings and magistrates is nothing else but what is only derivative, transferred, and committed to them in trust from the people to the common good of them all, in whom the power yet remains fundamentally, and cannot be taken from them without a violation of their natural birthright; and seeing that from hence Aristotle, and the best of political writers, have defined a king, 'him who governs to the

'good and profit of his people, and not for his own
'ends;' it follows from necessary causes that the
titles of sovereign lord, natural lord, and the like,
are either arrogancies or flatteries, not admitted by
emperors and kings of best note, and disliked by
the church both of Jews (Isa. xxvi. 13) and ancient
Christians, as appears by Tertullian and others.
Although generally the people of Asia, and with
them the Jews also, especially since the time they
chose a king against the advice and counsel of
God, are noted by wise authors much inclinable
to slavery.

Secondly, that to say, as is usual, the king hath
as good right to his crown and dignity as any man
to his inheritance, is to make the subject no better
than the king's slave, his chattel, or his possession
that may be bought and sold: and doubtless, if
hereditary title were sufficiently inquired, the best
foundation of it would be found but either in
courtesy or convenience. But suppose it to be of
right hereditary, what can be more just and legal,
if a subject for certain crimes be to forfeit by law
from himself and posterity all his inheritance to
the king, than that a king, for crimes proportional,
should forfeit all his title and inheritance to the
people? Unless the people must be thought created
all for him, he not for them, and they all in one
body inferior to him single; which were a kind
of treason against the dignity of mankind to affirm.

Thirdly, it follows that to say kings are ac-
countable to none but God, is the overturning of

all law and government. For if they may refuse
to give account, then all covenants made with
them at coronation, all oaths are in vain, and mere
mockeries; all laws which they swear to keep,
made to no purpose : for if the king fear not God,
(as how many of them do not,) we hold then our
lives and estates by the tenure of his mere grace
and mercy, as from a god, not a mortal magistrate ;
a position that none but court-parasites or men
besotted would maintain. Aristotle, therefore,
whom we commonly allow for one of the best
interpreters of nature and morality, writes in the
fourth of his Politics, chap. x., that 'monarchy
'unaccountable is the worst sort of tyranny, and
'least of all to be endured by free-born men.'

    *   *   *   *   *   *   *

Therefore kingdom and magistracy, whether
supreme or subordinate, is called 'a human or-
'dinance,' (1 Pet. ii. 13, &c.,) which we are there
taught is the will of God we should submit to, so
far as for the punishment of evil-doers, and the
encouragement of them that do well. 'Submit,'
saith he, 'as free men.' But to any civil power
unaccountable, unquestionable, and not to be resisted, no, not in wickedness and violent actions,
how can we submit as free men? 'There is no
'power but of God,' saith Paul ; (Rom. xiii.;) as
much as to say, God put it into man's heart to find
out that way at first for common peace and preservation, approving the exercise thereof; else it
contradicts Peter, who calls the same authority an

14

ordinance of man.   It must be also understood of
lawful and just power, else we read of great power
in the affairs and kingdoms of the world permitted
to the devil : for saith he to Christ, (Luke, iv. 6,)
‘ All this power will I give thee, and the glory of
‘ them, for it is delivered to me, and to whomsoever
‘ I will I give it : ’ neither did he lie, or Christ
gainsay what he affirmed ; for in the thirteenth of
the Revelation we read how the dragon gave to
the beast his power, his seat, and great authority : which beast so authorized most expound to
be the tyrannical powers and kingdoms of the
earth.   Therefore Saint Paul in the forecited chapter tells us that such magistrates he means as are
not a terror to the good, but to the evil ; such as
bear not the sword in vain, but to punish offenders,
and to encourage the good.

If such only be mentioned here as powers to be
obeyed, and our submission to them only required,
then doubtless those powers that do the contrary
are no powers ordained of God ; and by consequence no obligation laid upon us to obey or not
to resist them.   And it may be well observed, that
both these apostles, whenever they give this precept, express it in terms not concrete, but abstract,
as logicians are wont to speak ; that is, they
mention the ordinance, the power, the authority,
before the persons that execute it ; and what that
power is, lest we should be deceived, they describe
exactly.   So that if the power be not such, or the
person execute not such power, neither the one nor

the other is of God, but of the devil, and by consequence to be resisted. From this exposition
Chrysostom also, on the same place, dissents not ;
explaining that these words were not written in
behalf of a tyrant. And this is verified by David,
himself a king, and likeliest to be author of the
Psalm (xciv. 20) which saith, 'Shall the throne of
'iniquity have fellowship with thee?' And it
were worth the knowing,—since kings in these days,
and that by Scripture, boast the justness of their
title by holding it immediately of God, yet cannot
shew the time when God ever set on the throne
them or their forefathers, but only when the people
chose them ;—why by the same reason, since God
ascribes as oft to himself the casting down of
princes from the throne, it should not be thought
as lawful, and as much from God, when none are
seen to do it but the people, and that for just
causes. For if it needs must be a sin in them to
depose, it may as likely be a sin to have elected.
And contrary, if the people's act in election be
pleaded by a king as the act of God, and the most
just title to enthrone him, why may not the
people's act of rejection be as well pleaded by the
people as the act of God, and the most just reason
to depose him? So that we see the title and just
right of reigning or deposing, in reference to God,
is found in Scripture to be all one ; visible only in
the people, and depending merely upon justice and
demerit. Thus far hath been considered chiefly
the power of kings and magistrates ; how it was

and is originally the people's, and by them con-
ferred in trust only to be employed to the common
peace and benefit ; with liberty therefore and right
remaining in them to reassume it to themselves, if
by kings or magistrates it be abused ; or to dispose
of it by any alteration, as they shall judge most
conducing to the public good.

We may from hence with more ease and force
of argument determine what a tyrant is, and what
the people may do against him. A tyrant, whether
by wrong or by right coming to the crown, is he
who, regarding neither law nor the common good,
reigns only for himself and his faction : thus St.
Basil, among others, defines him. And because
his power is great, his will boundless and exor-
bitant, the fulfilling whereof is for the most part
accompanied with innumerable wrongs and oppressions of the people, murders, massacres, rapes,
adulteries, desolation and subversion of cities and
whole provinces ; look how great a good and happiness a just king is, so great a mischief is a tyrant ;
as he the public father of his country, so this the
common enemy. Against whom what the people
lawfully may do, as against a common pest and
destroyer of mankind, I suppose no man of clear
judgment need go further to be guided than by the
very principles of nature in him.

But because it is the vulgar folly of men to
desert their own reason, and shutting their eyes,
to think they see best with other men's, I shall
show, by such examples as ought to have most

weight with us, what hath been done in this case heretofore. The Greeks and Romans, as their prime authors witness, held it not only lawful but a glorious and heroic deed, rewarded publicly with statues and garlands, to kill an infamous tyrant at any time without trial; and but reason, that he who trod down all law should not be vouchsafed the benefit of the law. Insomuch that Seneca the tragedian brings in Hercules, the grand suppressor of tyrants, thus speaking :—

> Victima haud ulla amplior
> Potest, magisque opima mactari Jovi
> Quam rex iniquus.

> There can be slain
> No sacrifice to God more acceptable
> Than an unjust and wicked king.

But of these I name no more, lest it be objected they were heathen; and come to produce another sort of men, that had the knowledge of true religion. Among the Jews this custom of tyrant-killing was not unusual. First, Ehud, a man whom God had raised to deliver Israel from Eglon king of Moab, who had conquered and ruled over them eighteen years, being sent to him as an ambassador with a present, slew him in his own house. ' But he was a foreign prince, an enemy, ' and Ehud besides had special warrant from God.' To the first I answer, it imports not whether foreign or native : for no prince so native but professes to hold by law ; which when he himself overturns, breaking all the covenants and oaths

that gave title to his dignity, and were the bond and
alliance between him and his people, what differs
he from an outlandish king, or from an enemy?
For look how much right the king of Spain hath
to govern us at all, so much right hath the king of
England to govern us tyrannically. If he, though
not bound to us by any league, coming from Spain
in person to subdue us or to destroy us, might lawfully by the people of England either be slain in
fight or put to death in captivity, what hath a native
king to plead, bound by so many covenants, benefits,
and honours, to the welfare of his people, why he
through the contempt of all laws and parliaments,
the only tie of our obedience to him, for his own
will's sake, and a boasted prerogative unaccountable, after seven years' warring and destroying of
his best subjects, overcome, and yielded prisoner,
should think to scape unquestionable, as a thing
divine, in respect of whom so many thousand
Christians destroyed should lie unaccounted for,
polluting with their slaughtered carcasses all the
land over, and crying for vengeance against the
living that should have righted them? Who knows
not that there is a mutual bond of amity and
brotherhood between man and man over all the
world, neither is it the English sea that can sever
us from that duty and relation : a straiter bond
there is between fellow-subjects, neighbours, and
friends. But when any of these do one to another
so as hostility could do no worse, what doth the
law decree less against them than open enemies

and invaders? or if the law be not present or too
weak, what doth it warrant us to less than single
defence or civil war? and from that time forward
the law of civil defensive war differs nothing from
the law of foreign hostility. Nor is it distance of
place that makes enmity, but enmity that makes
distance. He, therefore, that keeps peace with
me, near or remote, of whatsoever nation, is to me,
as far as all civil and human offices, an Englishman and a neighbour: but if an Englishman, forgetting all laws, human, civil, and religious, offend
against life and liberty, to him offended, and to the
law in his behalf, though born in the same womb,
he is no better than a Turk, a Saracen, a heathen.
This is gospel, and this was ever law among
equals; how much rather then in force against
any king whatever, who in respect of the people is
confessed inferior and not equal: to distinguish,
therefore, of a tyrant by outlandish or domestic,
is a weak evasion. To the second, that he was an
enemy, I answer, what tyrant is not? yet Eglon
by the Jews had been acknowledged as their sovereign, they had served him eighteen years, as long
almost as we our William the Conqueror, in all
which he could not be so unwise a statesman but
to have taken of them oaths of fealty and allegiance; by which they made themselves his proper
subjects, as their homage and present sent by
Ehud testified. To the third, that he had special
warrant to kill Eglon in that manner, it cannot be
granted, because not expressed; it is plain that he

was raised by God to be a deliverer, and went on just principles, such as were then and ever held allowable to deal so by a tyrant that could no otherwise be dealt with.

Neither did Samuel, though a prophet, with his own hand abstain from Agag; a foreign enemy no doubt; but mark the reason : ' As thy sword hath ' made women childless ;' a cause that by the sentence of law itself nullifies all relations.   And as the law is between brother and brother, father and son, master and servant, wherefore not between king, or rather tyrant, and people?   And whereas Jehu had special command to slay Jehoram, a successive and hereditary tyrant, it seems not the less imitable for that ; for where a thing grounded so much on natural reason hath the addition of a command from God, what does it but establish the lawfulness of such an act?   Nor is it likely that God, who had so many ways of punishing the house of Ahab, would have sent a subject against his prince, if the fact in itself, as done to a tyrant, had been of bad example.   And if David refused to lift his hand against the Lord's anointed, the matter between them was not tyranny, but private enmity ; and David, as a private person, had been his own revenger, not so much the people's : but when any tyrant at this day can shew himself to be the Lord's anointed, the only mentioned reason why David withheld his hand, he may then, but not till then, presume on the same privilege.

We may pass, therefore, hence to Christian

times. And first, our Saviour himself, how much he favoured tyrants, and how much intended they should be found or honoured among Christians, declared his mind not obscurely; accounting their absolute authority no better than Gentilism, yea, though they flourished it over with the splendid name of benefactors; charging those that would be his disciples to usurp no such dominion; but that they who were to be of most authority among them should esteem themselves ministers and servants to the public: Matt. xx. 25: 'The princes 'of the Gentiles exercise lordship over them;' and Mark x. 42: 'They that seem to rule,' saith he, either slighting or accounting them no lawful rulers; 'but ye shall not be so, but the greatest 'among you shall be your servant.' And although he himself were the meekest, and came on earth to be so, yet to a tyrant we hear him not vouchsafe an humble word, but, 'Tell that fox,' Luke xiii. So far we ought to be from thinking that Christ and his gospel should be made a sanctuary for tyrants from justice, to whom his law before never gave such protection. And wherefore did his mother, the Virgin Mary, give such praise to God in her prophetic song, that he had now, by the coming of Christ, cut down dynastas, or proud monarchs, from the throne, if the church, when God manifests his power in them to do so, should rather choose all misery and vassalage to serve them, and let them still sit on their potent seats to be adored for doing mischief?

Surely it is not for nothing that tyrants, by a kind of natural instinct, both hate and fear none more than the true church and saints of God, as the most dangerous enemies and subverters of monarchy, though indeed of tyranny; hath not this been the perpetual cry of courtiers and court-prelates? whereof no likelier cause can be alleged but that they well discerned the mind and principles of most devout and zealous men, and indeed the very discipline of church, tending to the dissolution of all tyranny. No marvel then if since the faith of Christ received, in purer or impurer times, to depose a king and put him to death for tyranny hath been accounted so just and requisite that neighbour kings have both upheld and taken part in the action. And Ludovicus Pius, himself an emperor, and son of Charles the Great, being made judge (du Haillan is my author) between Milegast, king of the Vultzes, and his subjects, who had deposed him, gave his verdict for the subjects, and for him whom they had chosen in his room. Note here that the right of electing whom they please is, by the impartial testimony of an emperor, in the people: for, said he, 'A just prince ought to 'be preferred before an unjust, and the end of 'government before the prerogative.'

And Constantinus Leo, another emperor, in the Byzantine laws saith, 'That the end of a king is 'for the general good, which he not performing is 'but the counterfeit of a king.' And to prove that some of our own monarchs have acknowledged that their high office exempted them not from punishment, they had the sword of St. Edward borne before them by an officer, who was called earl of the palace, even at the times of their highest pomp and solemnities; to mind them, saith Matthew Paris, the best of our historians, ' that if they erred, the sword had power to restrain ' them.' And what restraint the sword comes to at length, having both edge and point, if any sceptic will doubt, let him feel. It is also affirmed from diligent search made in our ancient books of law, that the peers and barons of England had a legal right to judge the king: which was the cause most likely, (for it could be no slight cause,) that they were called his peers, or equals. This, however, may stand immovable, so long as man hath to deal with no better than man; that if our law judge all men to the lowest by their peers, it should, in all equity, ascend also, and judge the highest.

And so much I find both in our own and foreign story, that dukes, earls, and marquises were at first not hereditary, not empty and vain titles, but names of trust and office, and with the office ceasing; as induces me to be of opinion that every worthy man in parliament, (for the word baron imports no more,) might for the public good be thought a fit peer and judge of the king, without regard had to petty caveats and circumstances, the chief impediment in high affairs, and ever stood upon most by circumstantial men. Whence doubtless our ancestors who were not ignorant with what rights either nature or ancient constitution had endowed them, when oaths both at coronation and renewed in parliament would not serve, thought it no way illegal to depose and put to death their tyrannous kings. Insomuch that the parliament drew up a charge against Richard the Second, and the commons requested to have judgment decreed against him, that the realm might not be endangered. And Peter Martyr, a divine of foremost rank, on the third of Judges approves their doings. Sir Thomas Smith also, a protestant, and a statesman, in his Commonwealth of England, putting the question, 'whether it be lawful to rise 'against a tyrant;' answers, 'that the vulgar 'judge of it according to the event, and the learned 'according to the purpose of them that do it.'

But far before those days, Gildas, the most ancient of all our historians, speaking of those times wherein the Roman empire decaying quitted and relinquished what right they had by conquest to this island, and resigned it all into the people's hands, testifies that the people thus reinvested with their own original right, about the year 445, both elected them kings whom they thought best, (the first Christian British kings that ever reigned here since the Romans,) and by the same right, when they apprehended cause, usually deposed and put them to death. This is the most fundamental and ancient tenure that any king of England can produce or pretend to; in comparison of which, all other titles and pleas are but of yesterday. If any object that Gildas condemns the Britons for so doing, the answer is as ready; that he condemns them no more for so doing than he did before for choosing such; for, saith he, 'They anointed 'them kings not of God, but such as were more 'bloody than the rest.' Next, he condemns them not at all for deposing or putting them to death, but for doing it over hastily, without trial or well examining the cause, and for electing others worse in their room.

Thus we have here both domestic and most ancient examples, that the people of Britain have deposed and put to death their kings in those primitive Christian times. And to couple reason with example, if the church in all ages, primitive, Romish, or protestant, held it ever no less their duty than the power of their keys, though without express warrant of Scripture, to bring indifferently both king and peasant under the utmost rigour of their canons and censures ecclesiastical, even to the smiting him with a final excommunion, if he persist impenitent; what hinders but that the temporal law both may and ought, though without a special text or precedent, extend with like indifference the civil sword, to the cutting off, without exemption, him that capitally offends, seeing that justice and religion are from the same God, and works of justice ofttimes more acceptable? Yet because that some lately, with the tongues and arguments of malignant backsliders, have written that the proceedings now in parliament against the king are without precedent from any protestant state or kingdom, the examples which follow shall be all protestant, and chiefly presbyterian.

In the year 1546, the Duke of Saxony, Land-grave of Hesse, and the whole protestant league, raised open war against Charles the Fifth, their emperor, sent him a defiance, renounced all faith and allegiance toward him, and debated long in council whether they should give him so much as the title of Cæsar. Let all men judge what this wanted of deposing or of killing, but the power to do it.

In the year 1559, the Scots protestants claiming promise of their queen-regent for liberty of conscience, she answering that promises were not to be claimed of princes beyond what was commodious for them to grant, told her to her face in the parliament then at Stirling that if it were so they renounced their obedience; and soon after betook them to arms. Certainly, when allegiance is renounced, that very hour the king or queen is in effect deposed.

In the year 1564, John Knox, a most famous divine, and the reformer of Scotland to the presbyterian discipline, at a general assembly maintained openly, in a dispute against Lethington the secretary of state, that subjects might and ought to execute God's judgments upon their king; that the fact of Jehu and others against their king, having the ground of God's ordinary command to

put such and such offenders to death, was not
extraordinary, but to be imitated of all that preferred the honour of God to the affection of flesh
and wicked princes; that kings, if they offend
have no privilege to be exempted from the punish-
ments of law more than any other subject : so that
if the king be a murderer, adulterer, or idolater,
he should suffer, not as a king but as an offender ;
and this position he repeats again and again before
them. Answerable was the opinion of John Craig,
another learned divine, and that laws made by the
tyranny of princes, or the negligence of people,
their posterity might abrogate, and reform all
things according to the original institution of commonwealths. And Knox being commanded by
the nobility to write to Calvin and other learned
men for their judgments in that question, refused,
alleging that both himself was fully resolved in
conscience, and had heard their judgments, and
had the same opinion under handwriting of many
the most godly and most learned that he knew in
Europe ; that if he should move the question to
them again, what should he do but show his own
forgetfulness or inconstancy ? All this is far more
largely in the ecclesiastical history of Scotland,
(l. iv.) with many other passages to this effect all
the book over, set out with diligence by Scotsmen
of best repute among them at the beginning of
these troubles ; as if they laboured to inform us
what we were to do, and what they intended upon
the like occasion.

And to let the world know that the whole church and protestant state of Scotland in those purest times of reformation were of the same belief, three years after, they met in the field Mary their lawful and hereditary queen, took her prisoner, yielding before fight, kept her in prison, and the same year deposed her.

And four years after that, the Scots, in justification of their deposing Queen Mary, sent ambassadors to Queen Elizabeth, and in a written declaration alleged, that they had used towards her more lenity than she deserved; that their ancestors had heretofore punished their kings by death or banishment; that the Scots were a free nation, made king whom they freely chose, and with the same freedom unkinged him if they saw cause, by right of ancient laws and ceremonies yet remaining, and old customs yet among the highlanders in choosing the head of their clans or families; all which, with many other arguments, bore witness that regal power was nothing else but a mutual covenant or stipulation between king and people. These were Scotchmen and presbyterians: but what measure then have they lately offered, to think such liberty less beseeming us than themselves, presuming to put him upon us for a master whom their law scarce allows to be their own equal? If now then we hear them in another strain than heretofore in the purest times of their church, we may be confident it is the voice of faction speaking in them, not of truth and reformation. Which no less in

England than in Scotland, by the mouths of those
faithful witnesses commonly called puritans and
non-conformists, spake as clearly for the putting
down, yea, the utmost punishing of kings, as in
their several treatises may be read ; even from
the first reign of Elizabeth to these times. Insomuch that one of them, whose name was Gibson,
foretold King James he should be rooted out, and
conclude his race, if he persisted to uphold bishops.
And that very inscription, stamped upon the first
coins at his coronation, a naked sword in a hand,
with these words, '*Si mereor, in me*,' 'Against
' me, if I deserve,' not only manifested the judgment
of that state, but seemed also to presage the
sentence of divine justice in this event upon his
son.

In the year 1581, the states of Holland, in a
general assembly at the Hague, abjured all obedience and subjection to Philip king of Spain ; and
in a declaration justify their so doing ; for that by
his tyrannous government, against faith so many
times given and broken, he had lost his right to all
the Belgic provinces ; that therefore they deposed
him, and declared it lawful to choose another in
his stead. From that time to this, no state or
kingdom in the world hath equally prospered :
but let them remember not to look with an evil
and prejudicial eye upon their neighbours walking
by the same rule.

*   *   *   *   *   *   *

For as to this question in hand, what the people

15

by their just right may do in change of government, or of governor, we see it cleared sufficiently, besides other ample authority, even from the mouths of princes themselves. And surely they that shall boast, as we do, to be a free nation, and not have in themselves the power to remove or to abolish any governor, supreme or subordinate, with the government itself upon urgent causes, may please their fancy with a ridiculous and painted freedom, fit to cozen babies; but we are indeed under tyranny and servitude, as wanting that power, which is the root and source of all liberty, to dispose and economize in the land which God hath given them, as masters of family in their own house and free inheritance. Without which natural and essential power of a free nation, though bearing high their heads, they can in due esteem be thought no better than slaves and vassals born, in the tenure and occupation of another inheriting lord; whose government, though not illegal or intolerable, hangs over them as a lordly scourge, not as a free government; and therefore to be abrogated.

How much more justly then may they fling off tyranny, or tyrants; who being once deposed can be no more than private men, as subject to the reach of justice and arraignment as any other transgressors? And certainly if men, not to speak of heathen, both wise and religious, have done justice upon tyrants what way they could soonest, how much more mild and humane then is it, to give them fair and open trial; to teach lawless kings,

and all who so much adore them, that not mortal
man or his imperious will, but justice, is the only
true sovereign and supreme majesty upon earth.
Let men cease therefore out of faction and hypocrisy to make outcries and horrid things of things
so just and honourable. Though perhaps till now
no protestant state or kingdom can be alleged to
have openly put to death their king, which lately
some have written, and imputed to their great
glory ; much mistaking the matter. It is not,
neither ought to be, the glory of a protestant state
never to have put their king to death ; it is the
glory of a protestant king never to have deserved
death. And if the parliament and military council
do what they do without precedent, if it appear
their duty, it argues the more wisdom, virtue, and
magnanimity, that they know themselves able to
be a precedent to others ; who perhaps in future
ages, if they prove not too degenerate, will look
up with honour and aspire toward these exemplary and matchless deeds of their ancestors, as to
the highest top of their civil glory and emulation ;
which heretofore, in the pursuance of fame and
foreign dominion, spent itself vaingloriously abroad ;
but henceforth may learn a better fortitude, to dare
execute highest justice on them that shall by force
of arms endeavour the oppressing and bereaving of
religion and their liberty at home. That no unbridled potentate or tyrant, but to his sorrow, for
the future may presume such high and irresponsible
licence over mankind, to havoc and turn upside

down whole kingdoms of men, as though they were
no more in respect of his perverse will than a
nation of pismires.

As for the party called presbyterian, of whom I
believe very many to be good and faithful Christians, though misled by some of turbulent spirit, I
wish them, earnestly and calmly, not to fall off
from their first principles, nor to affect rigour and
superiority over men not under them ; not to com-
pel unforcible things, in religion especially, which
if not voluntary becomes a sin ; not to assist the
clamour and malicious drifts of men whom they
themselves have judged to be the worst of men,
the obdurate enemies of God and his church : nor
to dart against the actions of their brethren, for
want of other argument, those wrested laws and
scriptures thrown by prelates and malignants
against their own sides, which though they hurt
not otherwise, yet taken up by them to the con-
demnation of their own doings give scandal to all
men, and discover in themselves either extreme
passion or apostacy. Let them not oppose their
best friends and associates, who molest them not
at all, infringe not the least of their liberties,
unless they call it their liberty to bind other men's
consciences, but are still seeking to live at peace
with them and brotherly accord. Let them beware
an old and perfect enemy, who, though he hope by
sowing discord to make them his instruments, yet
cannot forbear a minute the open threatening of
his destined revenge upon them, when they have

served his purposes. Let them fear therefore, if
they be wise, rather what they have done already
than what remains to do, and be warned in time
that they put no confidence in princes whom
they have provoked, lest they be added to the
examples of those that miserably have tasted the
event.

Stories can inform them how Christiern the
Second, king of Denmark, not much above a
hundred years past, driven out by his subjects, and
received again upon new oaths and conditions,
broke through them all to his most bloody revenge;
slaying his chief opposers, when he saw his time,
both them and their children, invited to a feast for
that purpose. How Maximilian dealt with those
of Bruges, though by mediation of the German
princes reconciled to them by solemn and public
writings drawn and sealed. How the massacre at
Paris was the effect of that credulous peace which
the French protestants made with Charles IX.
their king : and that the main visible cause which
to this day hath saved the Netherlands from utter
ruin, was their final not believing the perfidious
cruelty which, as a constant maxim of state, hath
been used by the Spanish kings on their subjects
that have taken arms, and after trusted them ; as
no latter age but can testify, heretofore in Belgia
itself, and this very year in Naples. And to conclude with one past exception, though far more
ancient, David, whose sanctified prudence might
be alone sufficient, not to warrant us only, but to

instruct us, when once he had taken arms, never after that trusted Saul, though with tears and much relenting he twice promised not to hurt him. These instances, few of many, might admonish them, both English and Scotch, not to let their own ends, and the driving on of a faction, betray them blindly into the snare of those enemies whose revenge looks on them as the men who first began, fomented, and carried on, beyond the cure of any sound or safe accommodation, all the evil which hath since unavoidably befallen them and their king.

I have something also to the divines, though brief to what were needful; not to be disturbers of the civil affairs, being in hands better able and more belonging to manage them; but to study harder, and to attend the office of good pastors, knowing that he whose flock is least among them hath a dreadful charge, not performed by mount-ing twice into the chair with a formal preachment huddled up at the odd hours of a whole lazy week, but by incessant pains and watching, in season and out of season, from house to house, over the souls of whom they have to feed. Which if they ever well considered, how little leisure would they find to be the most pragmatical sidesmen of every popular tumult and sedition! and all this while are to learn what the true end and reason is of the gospel which they teach; and what a world it differs from the censorious and supercilious lording over conscience. It would be good also they

lived so as might persuade the people they hated
covetousness, which, worse than heresy, is idolatry;
hated pluralities, and all kind of simony; left
rambling from benefice to benefice, like ravenous
wolves seeking where they may devour the biggest.
Of which if some, well and warmly seated from the
beginning, be not guilty, it were good they held
not conversation with such as are. Let them be
sorry that, being called to assemble about reforming the church, they fell to progging and soliciting
the parliament, though they had renounced the
name of priests, for a new settling of their tithes
and oblations ; and double-lined themselves with
spiritual places of commodity beyond the possible
discharge of their duty. Let them assemble in
consistory with their elders and deacons, according
to ancient ecclesiastical rule, to the preserving of
church discipline, each in his several charge, and
not a pack of clergymen by themselves to belly-
cheer in their presumptuous Sion, or to promote
designs, abuse and gull the simple laity, and stir
up tumult, as the prelates did, for the maintenance
of their pride and avarice.

These things if they observe, and wait with
patience, no doubt but all things will go well
without their importunities or exclamations ; and
the printed letters which they send subscribed
with the ostentation of great characters and little
moment, would be more considerable than now
they are. But if they be the ministers of mammon
instead of Christ, and scandalize his church with

the filthy love of gain, aspiring also to sit the closest and the heaviest of all tyrants upon the conscience, and fall notoriously into the same sins whereof so lately and so loud they accused the prelates; as God rooted out those wicked ones immediately before, so will he root out them, their imitators; and to vindicate his own glory and religion will uncover their hypocrisy to the open world; and visit upon their own heads that 'Curse 'ye Meroz,' the very motto of their pulpits, where-with so frequently, not as Meroz but more like atheists, they have blasphemed the vengeance of God, and traduced the zeal of his people.

And that they be not what they go for, true ministers of the protestant doctrine, taught by those abroad, famous and religious men, who first re-formed the church, or by those no less zealous who withstood corruption and the bishops here at home, branded with the name of puritans and non-conformists, we shall abound with testimonies to make appear: that men may yet more fully know the difference between protestant divines and these pulpit-firebrands. 'Such is the state of things at 'this day that men neither can, nor will, nor in-'deed ought to endure longer the domination of you 'princes.'[1] 'Neither is Cæsar to make war as 'head of Christendom, protector of the church, 'defender of the faith; these titles being false and 'windy, and most kings being the greatest enemies

---

[1] 'Is est hodie rerum status,' &c.—Luther. Lib. contra rusticos apud Sleidan. l.

'to religion.'[1] What hinders then but that we
may depose or punish them? These also are
recited by Cochlæus in his Miscellanies to be the
words of Luther, or some other eminent divine
then in Germany, when the protestants there
entered into solemn covenant at Smalcaldia : ' Ut
' ora iis obturem,' etc. 'That I may stop their
'mouths, the pope and emperor are not born, but
' elected ; and may also be deposed, as hath been
' often done.' If Luther, or whoever else, thought
so, he could not stay there ; for the right of birth
or succession can be no privilege in nature to let
a tyrant sit irremovable over a nation freeborn,
without transforming that nation from the nature
and condition of men born free into natural,
hereditary, and successive slaves. Therefore he
saith further; 'To displace and throw down this ex-
'actor, this Phalaris, this Nero, is a work pleasing
' to God;' namely, for being such a one : which is
a moral reason. Shall then so slight a consideration as his hap to be not elective simply, but
by birth, which was a mere accident, overthrow
that which is moral, and make unpleasing to God
that which otherwise had so well pleased him?
Certainly not : for if the matter be rightly argued,
election, much rather than chance, binds a man to
content himself with what he suffers by his own
bad election. Though indeed neither one nor the
other binds any man, much less any people, to a

---

[1] 'Neque vero Cæsarem,' &c.—Lib. de Bello contra
Turcas, apud Sleid. l. xiv.

necessary sufferance of those wrongs and evils which they have ability and strength enough given them to remove.

' When kings reign perfidiously, and against the
' rule of Christ, they may according to the word of
' God be deposed.'[1] 'I know not how it comes to
' pass that kings reign by succession, unless it be
' with consent of the whole people.'[2] ' But when by
' suffrage and consent of the whole people, or the
' better part of them, a tyrant is deposed or put to
' death, God is the chief leader in that action.'[3]
' Now that we are so lukewarm in upholding
' public justice, we endure the vices of tyrants to
' reign now-a-days with impunity; justly therefore
' by them we are trod underfoot, and shall at length
' with them be punished. Yet ways are not wanting
' by which tyrants may be removed, but there wants
' public justice.'[4] 'Beware, ye tyrants! for now
' the gospel of Jesus Christ, spreading far and wide,
' will renew the lives of many to love innocence and
' justice; which if ye also shall do, ye shall be
' honoured. But if ye shall go on to rage and do
' violence, ye shall be trampled on by all men.'[5]
' When the Roman empire, or any other, shall be-
' gin to oppress religion, and we negligently suffer

---

1 ' Quando vero perfide,' &c.—Zwinglius, tom. i. articul. 42.

2 ' Mihi ergo compertum non est,' &c.—Ibid.

3 ' Quum vero consensu,' &c.—Ibid.

4 ' Nunc cum tam tepidi sumus,' &c.—Ibid.

5 ' Cavete vobis o tyranni.'—Ibid.

'it, we are as much guilty of religion so violated
'as the oppressors themselves.'[1]

'Now-a-days monarchs pretend always in their
'titles to be kings by the grace of God ; but how
'many of them to this end only pretend it, that they
'may reign without control !   For to what purpose
'is the grace of God mentioned in the title of kings,
'but that they may acknowledge no superior?   In
'the meanwhile God, whose name they use to
'support themselves, they willingly would tread
'under their feet.   It is therefore a mere cheat
'when they boast to reign by the grace of God.'[2]
'Earthly princes depose themselves, while they
'rise against God ; yea, they are unworthy to be
'numbered among men : rather it behoves us to
'spit upon their heads than to obey them.'[3]

'If a sovereign prince endeavour by arms to
'defend transgressors, to subvert those things which
'are taught in the word of God, they who are in
'authority under him ought first to dissuade him ;
'if they prevail not, and that he now bears himself
'not as a prince but as an enemy, and seeks to
'violate privileges and rights granted to inferior
'magistrates or commonalties, it is the part of pious
'magistrates, imploring first the assistance of God,

---

1 ' Romanum imperium imo quodque,' &c.—Zwinglius,
Epist. ad Conrad. Somium.

2 ' Hodie monarchæ semper in 'suis titulis,' &c.—Calvin
on Daniel, c. iv. v. 25.

3 ' Abdicant se terreni principes,' &c.—On Dan. c. vi. v.
22.

'rather to try all ways and means than to betray
'the flock of Christ to such an enemy of God : for
'they also are to this end ordained, that they may
'defend the people of God, and maintain those
'things which are good and just.   For to have
'supreme power lessens not the evil committed by
'that power, but makes it the less tolerable by how
'much the more generally hurtful.   Then certainly
'the less tolerable, the more unpardonably to be
'punished.'[1]   Of Peter Martyr we have spoke
before.   ' They whose part is to set up magistrates,
'may restrain them also from outrageous deeds, or
'pull them down ; but all magistrates are set up
'either by parliament or by electors, or by other
'magistrates ; they, therefore, who exalted them
'may lawfully degrade and punish them.'[2]

Of the Scots divines I need not mention others
than the famousest among them, Knox, and his
fellow-labourers in the reformation of Scotland ;
whose large treatise on this subject defends the
same opinion.   To cite them sufficiently, were to
insert their whole books, written purposely on this
argument, ' Knox's Appeal ;' and 'to the reader ;'
where he promises in a postscript that the book
which he intended to set forth, called ' The
' Second Blast of the Trumpet,' should maintain
more at large, that the same men most justly may
depose and punish him whom unadvisedly they

[1] ' Si princeps superior,' &c.—Bucer on Matth. c. v.

[2] ' Quorum est constituere magistratus,' &c.—Paræus in
Rom. xiii.

have elected, notwithstanding birth, succession, or any oath of allegiance. Among our own divines, Cartwright and Fenner, two of the learnedest, may in reason satisfy us what was held by the rest: Fenner, in his book of Theology, maintaining that they who have power, that is to say, a parliament, may either by fair means or by force depose a tyrant, whom he defines to be him that wilfully breaks all or the principal conditions made between him and the commonwealth.[1] And Cartwright, in a prefixed epistle, testifies his approbation of the whole book.

'Kings have their authority of the people, who 'may upon occasion reassume it to themselves.'[2] 'The people may kill wicked princes, as monsters 'and cruel beasts.'[3] 'When kings or rulers become 'blasphemers of God, oppressors and murderers of 'their subjects, they ought no more to be accounted 'kings, or lawful magistrates, but as private men 'to be examined, accused, and condemned and 'punished by the law of God ; and being convicted 'and punished by that law, it is not man's but God's 'doing.'[4] 'By the civil laws, a fool or idiot born, 'and so proved, shall lose the lands and inheritance 'whereto he is born, because he is not able to use 'them aright : and especially ought in no case be 'suffered to have the government of a whole nation ;

---

[1] Fen. Sac. Theolog. c. 13.
[2] Gilby de Obedientiâ, p. 25 and 105.
[3] England's Complaint against the Canons.
[4] Christopher Goodman of Obedience, c. x. p. 139.

'but there is no such evil can come to the common-
'wealth by fools and idiots as doth by the rage and
'fury of ungodly rulers; such, therefore, being
'without God, ought to have no authority over
'God's people, who by his word requireth the con-
'trary.'[1] 'No person is exempt by any law of
'God from this punishment: be he king, queen, or
'emperor, he must die the death; for God hath not
'placed them above others to transgress his laws as
'they list, but to be subject to them as well as
'others; and if they be subject to his laws, then to
'the punishment also, so much the more as their
'example is more dangerous.'[2] 'When magistrates
'cease to do their duty, the people are, as it were,
'without magistrates, yea, worse, and then God
'giveth the sword into the people's hand, and he
'himself is become immediately their head.'[3] 'If
'princes do right, and keep promise with you, then
'do you owe to them all humble obedience; if not,
'ye are discharged, and your study ought to be in
'this case how ye may depose and punish according
'to the law such rebels against God and oppressors
'of their country.'[4]

This Goodman was a minister of the English
church at Geneva, as Dudley Fenner was at
Middleburgh, or some other place in that country.
These were the pastors of those saints and con-
fessors, who, flying from the bloody persecution of
Queen Mary, gathered up at length their scattered

1 Christopher Goodman of Obedience, c. xi. p. 143, 144.
2 C. xiii. p. 184.   3 P. 185.   4 P. 190.

members into many congregations ; whereof some
in Upper, some in Lower Germany, part of them
settled at Geneva ; where this author having
preached on this subject, to the great liking of
certain learned and godly men who heard him,
was by them sundry times and with much instance
required to write more fully on that point. Who
thereupon took it in hand, and conferring with the
best learned in those parts, (among whom Calvin
was then living in the same city,) with their special
approbation he published this treatise, aiming
principally, as is testified by Whittingham in the
Preface, that his brethren of England, the protestants, might be persuaded in the truth of that
doctrine concerning obedience to magistrates.[1]

These were the true protestant divines of
England, our fathers in the faith we hold ; this
was their sense, who for so many years labouring
under prelacy, through all storms and persecutions
kept religion from extinguishing ; and delivered it
pure to us, till there arose a covetous and ambitious
generation of divines, (for divines they call themselves) who, feigning on a sudden to be new
converts and proselytes from episcopacy, under
which they had long temporised, opened their
mouths at length, in show against pluralities and
prelacy, but with intent to swallow them down
both ; gorging themselves like harpies on those
simonious places and preferments of their outed

---

[1] Whittingham in Prefat.

predecessors, as the quarry for which they hunted, not to plurality only but to multiplicity; for possessing which they had accused them their brethren, and aspiring under another title to the same authority and usurpation over the consciences of all men.

Of this faction divers reverend and learned divines (as they are styled in the phylactery of their own title-page) pleading the lawfulness of defensive arms against the king, in a treatise called 'Scrip-'ture and Reason,' seem in words to disclaim utterly the deposing of a king; but both the scripture, and the reasons which they use, draw consequences after them, which, without their bidding, conclude it lawful. For if by scripture, and by that especially to the Romans, which they most insist upon, kings, doing that which is contrary to St. Paul's definition of a magistrate, may be resisted, they may altogether with as much force of consequence be deposed or punished. And if by reason the unjust authority of kings 'may be 'forfeited in part, and his power be reassumed in 'part, either by the parliament or people, for the 'case in hazard and the present necessity,' as they affirm, p. 34, there can no scripture be alleged, no imaginable reason given, that necessity continuing, as it may always, and they in all prudence and their duty may take upon them to foresee it, why in such a case they may not finally amerce him with the loss of his kingdom, of whose amendment they have no hope. And if one wicked action persisted in against religion, laws, and liberties, may warrant us to thus much in part, why may not forty times as many tyrannies, by him committed, warrant us to proceed on restraining him, till the restraint become total? For the ways of justice are exactest proportion; if for one trespass of a king it require so much remedy or satisfaction, then for twenty more as heinous crimes it requires of him twenty-fold; and so proportionably, till it come to what is utmost among men. If in these proceedings against their king they may not finish, by the usual course of justice, what they have begun, they could not lawfully begin at all. For this golden rule of justice and morality, as well as of arithmetic, out of three terms which they admit, will as certainly and unavoidably bring out the fourth as any problem that ever Euclid or Apollonius made good by demonstration.

And if the parliament, being undeposable but by themselves, as is affirmed, p. 37, 38, might for his whole life, if they saw cause, take all power, authority, and the sword out of his hand, which in effect is to unmagistrate him, why might they not, being then themselves the sole magistrates in force, proceed to punish him, who, being lawfully deprived of all things that define a magistrate, can be now no magistrate to be degraded lower, but an offender to be punished? Lastly, whom they may defy, and meet in battle, why may they not as well prosecute by justice? For lawful war is but the execution of justice against them who refuse law.

16

Among whom if it be lawful (as they deny not, p. 19, 20,) to slay the king himself coming in front at his own peril, wherefore may not justice do that intendedly, which the chance of a defensive war might without blame have done casually, nay, purposely, if there it find him among the rest? They ask, p. 19, 'By what rule of conscience or 'God a state is bound to sacrifice religion, laws, 'and liberties, rather than a prince defending such 'as subvert them, should come in hazard of his 'life.' And I ask by what conscience, or divinity, or law, or reason, a state is bound to leave all these sacred concernments under a perpetual hazard and extremity of danger, rather than cut off a wicked prince, who sits plotting day and night to subvert them.

They tell us that the law of nature justifies any man to defend himself, even against the king in person : let them shew us then why the same law may not justify much more a state or whole people to do justice upon him against whom each private man may lawfully defend himself; seeing all kind of justice done is a defence to good men, as well as a punishment to bad; and justice done upon a tyrant is no more but the necessary self-defence of a whole commonwealth. To war upon a king that his instruments may be brought to condign punishment, and thereafter to punish them the instruments, and not to spare only, but to defend and honour him the author, is the strangest piece of justice to be called Christian, and the strangest piece of reason to be called human, that by men of reverence and learning, as their style imports them, ever yet was vented. They maintain in the third and fourth section, that a judge or inferior magistrate is anointed of God, is his minister, hath the sword in his hand, is to be obeyed by St. Peter's rule, as well as the supreme, and without difference anywhere expressed: and yet will have us fight against the supreme till he remove and punish the inferior magistrate; (for such were greatest delinquents;) whereas by scripture, and by reason, there can no more authority be shewn to resist the one than the other; and altogether as much, to punish or depose the supreme himself, as to make war upon him, till he punish or deliver up his inferior magistrates, whom in the same terms we are commanded to obey, and not to resist.

Thus while they, in a cautious line or two here and there stuffed in, are only verbal against the pulling down or punishing of tyrants, all the scripture and the reason which they bring, is in every leaf direct and rational, to infer it altogether as lawful, as to resist them. And yet in all their sermons, as hath by others been well noted, they went much further. For divines, if ye observe them, have their postures and their motions no less expertly, and with no less variety, than they that practise feats in the Artillery-ground. Sometimes they seem furiously to march on, and presently march counter; by and by they stand, and then retreat; or if need be, can face about, or wheel in a whole body, with that cunning and dexterity as is almost unperceivable, to wind themselves by shifting ground into places of more advantage. And providence only must be the drum, providence the word of command, that calls them from above, but always to some larger benefice, or acts them into such or such figures and promotions. At their turns and doublings no men readier, to the right, or to the left ; for it is their turns which they serve chiefly ; herein only singular, that with them there is no certain hand right or left, but as their own commodity thinks best to call it. But if there come a truth to be defended, which to them and their interest of this world seems not so profitable, straight these nimble motionists can find not even legs to stand upon ; and are no more of use to reformation thoroughly performed, and not superficially, or to the advancement of truth, (which among mortal men is always in her progress,) than if on a sudden they were struck maim and crippled. Which the better to conceal, or the more to countenance by a general conformity to their own limping, they would have scripture, they would have reason also made to halt with them for company ; and would put us off with impotent conclusions, lame and shorter than the premises.

In this posture they seem to stand with great zeal and confidence on the wall of Sion ; but like Jebusites, not like Israelites, or Levites : blind also as well as lame, they discern not David from Adonibezec : but cry him up for the Lord's anointed, whose thumbs and great toes not long

before they had cut off upon their pulpit cushions.
Therefore he who is our only King, the Root of
David, and whose kingdom is eternal righteousness,
with all those that war under him, whose happiness
and final hopes are laid up in that only just and
rightful kingdom, (which we pray incessantly may
come soon, and in so praying wish hasty ruin and
destruction to all tyrants,) even he our immortal
King, and all that love him, must of necessity have
in abomination these blind and lame defenders of
Jerusalem ; as the soul of David hated them, and
forbid them entrance into God's house, and his
own.   But as to those before them, which I cited
first (and with an easy search, for many more
might be added) as they there stand, without more
in number, being the best and chief of protestant
divines, we may follow them for faithful guides,
and without doubting may receive them, as witnesses abundant of what we here affirm concerning tyrants.   And indeed I find it generally the
clear and positive determination of them all, (not
prelatical, or of this late faction subprelatical,) who
have written on this argument ; that to do justice
on a lawless king is to a private man unlawful ; to
an inferior magistrate lawful : or if they were
divided in opinion, yet greater than these here alleged, or of more authority in the church, there can
be none produced.

　If any one shall go about, by bringing other
testimonies to disable these, or by bringing these
against themselves in other cited passages of their
books, he will not only fail to make good that false

and impudent assertion of those mutinous ministers,
that the deposing and punishing of a king or tyrant
'is against the constant judgment of all protestant
'divines,' it being quite the contrary; but will prove
rather what perhaps he intended not, that the judgment of divines, if it be so various and inconstant to
itself, is not considerable, or to be esteemed at all.
Ere which be yielded, as I hope it never will, these
ignorant assertors in their own art will have proved
themselves more and more not to be protestant
divines, whose constant judgment in this point
they have so audaciously belied, but rather to be a
pack of hungry church-wolves, who in the steps of
Simon Magus their father, following the hot scent of
double livings and pluralities, advowsons, donatives,
inductions, and augmentations, though uncalled to
the flock of Christ, but by the mere suggestion of
their bellies, like those priests of Bel whose pranks
Daniel found out, have got possesion or rather
seized upon the pulpit, as the stronghold and for-
tress of their sedition and rebellion against the
civil magistrate. Whose friendly and victorious
hand having rescued them from the bishops, their
insulting lords, fed them plenteously both in public
and in private, raised them to be high and rich of
poor and base; only suffered not their covetousness and fierce ambition (which as the pit that sent
out their fellow-locusts hath been ever bottomless
and boundless) to interpose in all things, and over
all persons, their impetuous ignorance and importunity.

EIKONOKLASTES

IN ANSWER TO A BOOK ENTITLED
'EIKON BASILIKE, THE PORTRAI-
'TURE OF HIS SACRED MAJESTY IN
'HIS SOLITUDES AND SUFFERINGS.'
PUBLISHED BY AUTHORITY (1649).

'As a roaring lion and a ranging bear, so is a wicked ruler
'over the poor people.
'The prince that wanteth understanding is also a great
'oppressor; but he that hateth covetousness shall
'prolong his days.
'A man that doth violence to the blood of any person
'shall flee to the pit; let no man stay him.'—Prov.
xxviii. 15, 16, 17.

'Regium imperium, quod initio conservandæ libertatis
'atque augendæ reipublicæ causa fuerat, in superbiam
'dominationemque se convertit.
'Regibus boni quam mali suspectiores sunt, semperque
'his aliena virtus formidolosa est.
'Impune quælibet facere, id est regem esse.'—Sallust.

The following extract is the second of twenty-eight chapters
in which 'Eikon Basilike' is reviewed in detail.

THIS next chapter is a penitent confession of the king, and the strangest, if it be well weighed, that ever was auricular. For he repents here of giving his consent, though most unwillingly, to the most seasonable and solemn piece of justice that had been done of many years in the land : but his sole conscience thought the contrary. And thus was the welfare, the safety, and, within a little, the unanimous demand of three populous nations, to have attended still on the singularity of one man's opinionated conscience ; if men had always been so tame and spiritless, and had not unexpectedly found the grace to understand that if his conscience were so narrow and peculiar to itself it was not fit his authority should be so ample and universal over others : for certainly a private conscience sorts not with a public calling, but declares that person rather meant by nature for a private fortune. And this also we may take for truth, that he whose conscience thinks it sin to put to death a capital offender, will as oft think it meritorious to kill a righteous person.

But let us hear what the sin was that lay so sore

upon him and, as one of his prayers given to Dr. Juxon testifies, to the very day of his death ; it was his signing the bill of Strafford's execution ; a man whom all men looked upon as one of the boldest and most impetuous instruments that the king had to advance any violent or illegal design. He had ruled Ireland, and some parts of England, in an arbitrary manner ; had endeavoured to subvert fundamental laws, to subvert parliaments, and to incense the king against them ; he had also endea- voured to make hostility between England and Scotland : he had counselled the king to call over that Irish army of papists, which he had cunningly raised, to reduce England, as appeared by good testimony then present at the consultation : for which and many other crimes alleged and proved against him in twenty-eight articles, he was con- demned of high-treason by the parliament.

The commons by far the greater number cast him : the lords, after they had been satisfied in a full discourse by the king's solicitor, and the opinions of many judges delivered in their house, agreed likewise to the sentence of treason. The people universally cried out for justice. None were his friends but courtiers and clergymen, the worst, at that time, and most corrupted sort of men ; and court ladies, not the best of women ; who when they grow to that insolence as to appear active in state affairs, are the certain sign of a disso- lute, degenerate, and pusillanimous commonwealth. Last of all, the king, or rather first, for these

were but his apes, was not satisfied in conscience
to condemn him of high-treason ; and declared to
both houses 'that no fears or respects whatsoever
'should make him alter that resolution founded
'upon his conscience.' Either then his resolution
was indeed not founded upon his conscience, or his
conscience received better information, or else
both his conscience and this his strong resolution
struck sail, notwithstanding these glorious words,
to his stronger fear ; for within a few days after,
when the judges, at a privy-council, and four of his
elected bishops had picked the thorn out of his
conscience, he was at length persuaded to sign the
bill for Strafford's execution. And yet perhaps
that it wrung his conscience to condemn the earl
of high-treason is not unlikely ; not because he
thought him guiltless of highest treason, had half
those crimes been committed against his own private interest or person, as appeared plainly by his
charge against the six members ; but because he
knew himself a principal in what the earl was but
his accessory, and thought nothing treason against
the commonwealth, but against himself only.

Had he really scrupled to sentence that for
treason which he thought not treasonable, why did
he seem resolved by the judges and the bishops ?
and if by them resolved, how comes the scruple
here again ? It was not then, as he now pretends,
'the importunities of some, and the fear of many,'
which made him sign, but the satisfaction given him
by those judges and ghostly fathers of his own

choosing. Which of him shall we believe? for he
seems not one, but double; either here we must
not believe him professing that his satisfaction was
but seemingly received and out of fear, or else we
may as well believe that the scruple was no real
scruple as we can believe him here against himself before, that the satisfaction then received was
no real satisfaction. Of such a variable and fleet-
ing conscience what hold can be taken?

But that indeed it was a facile conscience, and
could dissemble satisfaction when it pleased, his
own ensuing actions declared; being soon after
found to have the chief hand in a most detested
conspiracy against the parliament and kingdom, as
by letters and examinations of Percy, Goring, and
other conspirators came to light; that his intention
was to rescue the Earl of Strafford, by seizing on
the Tower of London; to bring up the English
army out of the North, joined with eight thousand
Irish papists raised by Strafford, and a French
army to be landed at Portsmouth, against the
parliament and their friends. For which purpose
the king, though requested by both houses to dis-
band those Irish papists, refused to do it, and kept
them still in arms to his own purposes. No marvel
then if being as deeply criminous as the earl himself it stung his conscience to adjudge to death
those misdeeds whereof himself had been the chief
author: no marvel though instead of blaming and
detesting his ambition, his evil counsel, his violence,
and oppression of the people, he fall to praise his

great abilities; and with scholastic flourishes, beneath the decency of a king, compares him to the sun, which in all figurative use and significance bears allusion to a king, not to a subject: no marvel though he knit contradictions as close as words can lie together, 'not approving in his 'judgment,' and yet approving in his subsequent reason all that Strafford did, as 'driven by the 'necessity of times, and the temper of that people;' for this excuses all his misdemeanors. Lastly, no marvel that he goes on building many fair and pious conclusious upon false and wicked premises, which deceive the common reader, not well discerning the antipathy of such connexions: but this is the marvel, and may be the astonishment, of all that have a conscience, how he durst in the sight of God (and with the same words of contrition wherewith David repents the murdering of Uriah) repent his lawful compliance to that just act of not saving him whom he ought to have delivered up to speedy punishment; though himself the guiltier of the two.

If the deed were so sinful, to have put to death so great a malefactor, it would have taken much doubtless from the heaviness of his sin, to have told God in his confession how he laboured, what dark plots he had contrived, into what a league entered, and with what conspirators, against his parliament and kingdoms, to have rescued from the claim of justice so notable and so dear an instrument of tyranny; which would have been a story, no doubt, as pleasing in the ears of heaven as all these equivocal repentances. For it was fear, and nothing. else, which made him feign before both the scruple and the satisfaction of his conscience, that is to say, of his mind : his first fear pretended conscience, that he might be borne with to refuse signing ; his latter fear, being more urgent, made him find a conscience both to sign and to be satisfied. As for repentance, it came not on him till a long time after ; when he saw 'he could have suffered nothing more, though he 'had denied that bill.' For how could he understandingly repent of letting that be treason which the parliament and whole nation so judged ? This was that which repented him, to have given up to just punishment so stout a champion of his designs, who might have been so useful to him in his following civil broils. It was a worldly repentance, not a conscientious ; or else it was a strange tyranny which his conscience had got over him, to vex him like an evil spirit for doing one act of justice, and by that means to 'fortify his resolution' from ever doing so any more. That mind must needs be irrecoverably depraved, which either by chance or importunity tasting but once of one just deed, spatters at it, and abhors the relish ever after.

To the Scribes and Pharisees woe was denounced by our Saviour, for straining at a gnat and swallowing a camel, though a gnat were to be strained at : but to a conscience with whom one good is so hard to pass down as to endanger almost a choking, and bad deeds without number, though as big and bulky as the ruin of three kingdoms, go down currently without straining, certainly a far greater woe appertains. If his conscience were come to that unnatural dyscrasy, as to digest poison and to keck at wholesome food, it was not for the parliament or any of his kingdoms to feed with him any longer. Which to conceal he would persuade us that the parliament also in their conscience escaped not 'some touches of remorse,' for putting Strafford to death, in forbidding it by an after-act to be a precedent for the future. But, in a fairer construction, that act implied rather a desire in them to pacify the king's mind, whom they perceived by this means quite alienated : in the meanwhile not imagining that this after-act should be retorted on them to tie up justice for the time to come upon like occasion, whether this were made a precedent or not, no more than the want of such a precedent, if it had been wanting, had been available to hinder this.

But how likely is it that this after-act argued in the parliament their least repenting for the death of Strafford, when it argued so little in the king himself ; who, notwithstanding this after-act, which had his own hand and concurrence, if not his own instigation, within the same year accused of high-treason no less than six members at once for the same pretended crimes which his conscience would not yield to think treasonable in the earl ? So that this his subtle argument to fasten a repenting and, by that means a guiltiness of Strafford's death upon the parliament, concludes upon his own head; and shows us plainly that either nothing in his judgment was treason against the commonwealth, but only against the king's person, (a tyrannical principle), or that his conscience was a perverse and prevaricating conscience, to scruple that the commonwealth should punish for treasonous in one eminent offender that which he himself sought so vehemently to have punished in six guiltless persons. If this were 'that touch of con-'science, which he bore with greater regret' than for any sin committed in his life, whether it were that proditory aid sent to Rochelle and religion abroad, or that prodigality of shedding blood at home, to a million of his subjects' lives not valued in comparison to one Strafford; we may consider yet at last, what true sense and feeling could be in that conscience, and what fitness to be the masterconscience of three kingdoms.

But the reason why he labours that we should take notice of so much 'tenderness and regret in 'his soul for having any hand in Strafford's death,' is worth the marking ere we conclude: 'he hoped 'it would be some evidence before God and man to 'all posterity, that he was far from bearing that 'vast load and guilt of blood' laid upon him by others: which hath the likeness of a subtle dissimulation; bewailing the blood of one man, his commodious instrument, put to death most justly, though by him unwillingly, that we might think him too tender to shed willingly the blood of those thousands whom he counted rebels. And thus by dipping voluntarily his finger's end, yet with show of great remorse, in the blood of Strafford, whereof all men clear him, he thinks to scape that sea of innocent blood, wherein his own guilt inevitably hath plunged him all over. And we may well perceive to what easy satisfactions and purgations he had inured his secret conscience, who thought by such weak policies and ostentations as these to gain belief and absolution from understanding men.

* * * * * * *

17

THE READY AND EASY WAY TO ESTABLISH A FREE COMMONWEALTH

AND THE EXCELLENCE THEREOF, COMPARED WITH THE INCONVENIENCES AND DANGERS OF READMITTING KINGSHIP IN THIS NATION. (1660.)

Et nos
Consilium dedimus Sullæ, demus populo nunc.

THE READY AND EASY WAY TO ESTABLISH A FREE COMMON-WEALTH.

ALTHOUGH since the writing of this treatise the face of things hath had some change, writs for new elections have been recalled, and the members at first chosen re-admitted from exclusion; yet not a little rejoicing to hear declared the resolution of those who are in power, tending to the establishment of a free commonwealth, and to remove, if it be possible, this noxious humour of returning to bondage, instilled of late by some deceivers, and nourished from bad principles and false apprehensions among too many of the people; I thought best not to suppress what I had written, hoping that it may now be of much more use and concernment to be freely published, in the midst of our elections to a free parliament, or their sitting to consider freely of the government; whom it behoves to have all things represented to them that may direct their judgment therein; and I never read of any state, scarce of any tyrant, grown so incurable as to refuse counsel from any in a time of public deliberation, much less to be offended. If their absolute determination be to enthral us, before so long a Lent of servitude they may permit us a little shroving-time first, wherein to speak freely, and take our leaves of liberty. And because in the former edition, through haste, many faults escaped, and many books were suddenly dispersed ere the note to mend them could be sent, I took the opportunity from this occasion to revise and somewhat to enlarge the whole discourse, especially that part which argues for a perpetual senate. The treatise thus revised and enlarged is as follows :

The Parliament of England, assisted by a great number of the people who appeared and stuck to them faithfulest in defence of religion and their civil liberties, judging kingship by long experience a government unnecessary, burdensome, and dangerous, justly and magnanimously abolished it, turning regal bondage into a free commonwealth, to the admiration and terror of our emulous neighbours. They took themselves not bound by the light of nature or religion to any former covenant, from which the king himself, by many forfeitures of a latter date or discovery, and our own longer consideration thereon, had more and more unbound us, both to himself and his posterity ; as hath been ever the justice and the prudence of all wise nations that have ejected tyranny. They covenanted ' to ' preserve the king's person and authority, in the ' preservation of the true religion and our liberties ;'

not in his endeavouring to bring in upon our consciences a popish religion, upon our liberties
thraldom, upon our lives destruction, by his
occasioning, if not complotting, as was after discovered, the Irish massacre, his fomenting and
arming the rebellion, his covert leaguing with the
rebels against us, his refusing, more than seven
times, propositions most just and necessary to the
true religion and our liberties, tendered him by
the parliament both of England and Scotland.
They made not their covenant concerning him
with no difference between a king and a God ; or
promised him, as Job did to the Almighty, ' to
' trust in him though he slay us : ' they understood
that the solemn engagement, wherein we all forswore
kingship, was no more a breach of the covenant
than the covenant was of the protestation before,
but a faithful and prudent going on both in words
well weighed and in the true sense of the covenant
' without respect of persons,' when we could not
serve two contrary masters, God and the king, or
the king and that more supreme law, sworn in the
first place to maintain our safety and our liberty.
They knew the people of England to be a free
people, themselves the representers of that freedom ;
and although many were excluded, and as many
fled (so they pretended) from tumults to Oxford,
yet they were left a sufficient number to act in
parliament, therefore not bound by any statute of
preceding parliaments, but by the law of nature
only, which is the only law of laws truly and

properly to all mankind fundamental, the beginning and the end of all government ; to which no parliament or people that will throughly reform, but may and must have recourse, as they had, and must yet have, in church reformation (if they throughly intend it) to evangelic rules ; not to ecclesiastical canons, though never so ancient, so ratified and established in the land by statutes which for the most part are mere positive laws, neither natural nor moral, and so by any parliament, for just and serious considerations, without scruple to be at any time repealed.

If others of their number in these things were under force, they were not, but under free conscience ; if others were excluded by a power which they could not resist, they were not therefore to leave the helm of government in no hands, to discontinue their care of the public peace and safety, to desert the people in anarchy and confusion, no more than when so many of their members left them as made up in outward formality a more legal parliament of three estates against them. The best affected also and best principled of the people stood not numbering or computing on which side were most voices in parliament, but on which side appeared to them most reason, most safety, when the house divided upon main matters. What was well mentioned and advised, they examined not whether fear or persuasion carried it in the vote, neither did they measure votes and counsels by the intentions of

them that voted ; knowing that intentions either
are but guessed at, or not soon enough known ;
and although good, can neither make the deed
such, nor prevent the consequence from being bad.
Suppose bad intentions in things otherwise well
done ; what was well done was by them who so
thought not the less obeyed or followed in the
state ; since in the church, who had not rather
follow Iscariot or Simon the magician, though to
covetous ends, preaching, than Saul, though in the
uprightness of his heart, persecuting the gospel ?

Safer they therefore judged what they thought
the better counsels, though carried on by some
perhaps to bad ends, than the worse by others,
though endeavoured with best intentions. And
yet they were not to learn that a greater number
might be corrupt within the walls of a parliament,
as well as of a city ; whereof in matters of nearest
concernment all men will be judges ; nor easily
permit that the odds of voices in their greatest
council shall more endanger them by corrupt or
credulous votes than the odds of enemies by open
assaults ; judging that most voices ought not
always to prevail, where main matters are in
question. If others hence will pretend to disturb
all counsels, what is that to them who pretend
not, but are in real danger ? not they only so
judging, but a great though not the greatest
number of their chosen patriots, who might be
more in weight than the others in numbers ; there
being in number little virtue, but by weight and

measure wisdom working all things; and the dangers on either side they seriously thus weighed.

From the treaty, short fruits of long labours, and seven years' war; security for twenty years, if we can hold it; reformation in the church for three years: then put to shift again with our vanquished master. His justice, his honour, his conscience declared quite contrary to ours; which would have furnished him with many such evasions as in a book entitled 'An Inquisition for Blood' soon after were not concealed : bishops not totally removed, but left, as it were, in ambush, a reserve, with ordination in their sole power; their lands already sold, not to be alienated, but rented, and the sale of them called 'sacrilege;' delinquents, few of many brought to condign punishment; accessories punished, the chief author above pardon, though after utmost resistance vanquished, not to give, but to receive, laws; yet besought, treated with, and to be thanked for his gracious concessions, to be honoured, worshipped, glorified.

If this we swore to do, with what righteousness in the sight of God, with what assurance that we bring not by such an oath the whole sea of blood-guiltiness upon our heads ? If on the other side we prefer a free government, though for the present not obtained, yet all those suggested fears and difficulties, as the event will prove, easily overcome, we remain finally secure from the exasperated regal power, and out of snares; shall retain the best part of our liberty, which is our religion, and the civil part will be from these who defer us much more easily recovered, being neither so subtle nor so awful as a king reinthroned. Nor were their actions less both at home and abroad than might become the hopes of a glorious rising common-wealth: nor were the expressions both of army and people, whether in their public declarations or several writings, other than such as testified a spirit in this nation no less noble and well-fitted to the liberty of a commonwealth than in the ancient Greeks or Romans. Nor was the heroic cause unsuccessfully defended to all Christendom, against the tongue of a famous and thought in-vincible adversary; nor the constancy and fortitude that so nobly vindicated our liberty, our victory at once against two the most prevailing usurpers over mankind, superstition and tyranny, unpraised or uncelebrated in a written monument, likely to outlive detraction, as it hath hitherto convinced or silenced not a few of our detractors, especially in parts abroad.

After our liberty and religion thus prosperously fought for, gained, and many years possessed, except in those unhappy interruptions which God hath removed; now that nothing remains but in all reason the certain hopes of a speedy and im-mediate settlement for ever in a firm and free commonwealth, for this extolled and magnified nation, regardless both of honour won or deliver-ances vouchsafed from heaven, to fall back, or rather to creep back, so poorly as it seems the multitude would, to their once abjured and detested thraldom of kingship, to be ourselves the slanderers of our own just and religious deeds, though done by some to covetous and ambitious ends, yet not therefore to be stained with their infamy, or they to asperse the integrity of others ; and yet these now by revolting from the conscience of deeds well done, both in church and state, to throw away and forsake, or rather to betray a just and noble cause for the mixture of bad men who have ill-managed and abused it, (which had our fathers done heretofore, and on the same pretence deserted true religion, what had long ere this become of our gospel, and all protestant reformation so much intermixed with the avarice and ambition of some reformers ?) and by thus relapsing to verify all the bitter predictions of our triumphing enemies, who will now think they wisely discerned and justly censured both us and all our actions as rash, rebellious, hypocritical, and impious ; not only argues a strange degenerate contagion suddenly spread among us, fitted and prepared for new slavery, but will render us a scorn and derision to all our neighbours.

And what will they at best say of us, and of the whole English name, but scoffingly, as of that foolish builder mentioned by our Saviour, who began to build a tower, and was not able to finish it? Where is this goodly tower of a commonwealth, which the English boasted they would build to overshadow kings, and be another Rome in the west? The foundation indeed they laid gallantly, but fell into a worse confusion, not of tongues but of factions, than those at the tower of Babel; and have left no memorial of their work behind them remaining but in the common laughter of Europe. Which must needs redound the more to our shame, if we but look on our neighbours the United Provinces, to us inferior in all outward advantages; who notwithstanding, in the midst of greater difficulties, courageously, wisely, constantly went through with the same work, and are settled in all the happy enjoyments of a potent and flourishing republic to this day.

Besides this, if we return to kingship, and soon repent, (as undoubtedly we shall, when we begin to find the old encroachment coming on by little and little upon our consciences, which must necessarily proceed from king and bishop united inseparably in one interest,) we may be forced perhaps to fight over again all that we have fought, and spend over again all that we have spent, but are never like to attain thus far as we are now advanced to the recovery of our freedom, never to have it in possession as we now have it, never to be vouchsafed hereafter the like mercies and signal assistances from Heaven in our cause, if by our ingrateful backsliding we make these fruitless; flying now to regal concessions from his divine condescensions and gracious answers to our once importuning prayers against the tyranny which we then groaned under; making vain and viler than dirt the blood of so many thousand faithful and valiant Englishmen, who left us in this liberty, bought with their lives ; losing by a strange after-game of folly all the battles we have won, together with all Scotland as to our conquest, hereby lost, which never any of our kings could conquer, all the treasure we have spent, not that corruptible treasure only, but that far more precious of all our late miraculous deliverances ; treading back again with lost labour all our happy steps in the progress of reformation, and most pitifully depriving our-selves the instant fruition of that free government which we have so dearly purchased, a free common-wealth, not only held by wisest men in all ages the noblest, the manliest, the equallest, the justest government, the most agreeable to all due liberty and proportioned equality, both human, civil, and Christian, most cherishing to virtue and true reli-gion, but also (I may say it with greatest proba-bility) plainly commended, or rather enjoined, by our Saviour himself to all Christians, not without remarkable disallowance and the brand of Genti-lism upon kingship.

God in much displeasure gave a king to the Israelites, and imputed it a sin to them that they sought one ; but Christ apparently forbids his dis-ciples to admit of any such heathenish government : ' The kings of the Gentiles,' saith he, ' exercise ' lordship over them, and they that exercise autho- ' rity upon them are called benefactors : but ye shall ' not be so ; but he that is greatest among you,

'let him be as the younger ; and he that is chief, as
'he that serveth.' The occasion of these his words
was the ambitious desire of Zebedee's two sons to
be exalted above their brethren in his kingdom,
which they thought was to be ere long upon earth.
That he speaks of civil government, is manifest by
the former part of the comparison, which infers the
other part to be always in the same kind. And
what government comes nearer to this precept of
Christ, than a free commonwealth ; wherein they
who are the greatest, are perpetual servants and
drudges to the public at their own cost and charges,
neglect their own affairs, yet are not elevated above
their brethren ; live soberly in their families, walk
the street as other men, may be spoken to freely,
familiarly, friendly, without adoration ? Whereas
a king must be adored like a demigod, with a dissolute and haughty court about him, of vast expense
and luxury, masks and revels, to the debauching of
our prime gentry, both male and female ; not in
their pastimes only but in earnest, by the loose
employments of court-service which will be then
thought honourable.

*   *   *   *   *   *   *

It may be well wondered that any nation,
styling themselves free, can suffer any man to pretend hereditary right over them as their lord ;
whenas, by acknowledging that right, they conclude
themselves his servants and his vassals, and so re-
nounce their own freedom. Which how a people
and their leaders especially can do, who have

fought so gloriously for liberty; how they can change their noble words and actions, heretofore so becoming the majesty of a free people, into the base necessity of court flatteries and prostrations, is not only strange and admirable, but lamentable to think on. That a nation should be so valorous and courageous to win their liberty in the field, and when they have won it, should be so heartless and unwise in their counsels as not to know how to use it, value it, what to do with it, or with themselves; but after ten or twelve years' prosperous war and contestation with tyranny, basely and besottedly to run their necks again into the yoke which they have broken, and prostrate all the fruits of their victory for nought at the feet of the vanquished, besides our loss of glory, and such an example as kings or tyrants never yet had the like to boast of, will be an ignominy, if it befall us, that never yet befell any nation possessed of their liberty; worthy indeed themselves, whatsoever they be, to be for ever slaves, but that part of the nation which consents not with them, as I persuade me of a great number, far worthier than by their means to be brought into the same bondage.

Considering these things so plain, so rational, I cannot but yet further admire on the other side how any man who hath the true principles of justice and religion in him can presume or take upon him to be a king and lord over his brethren, whom he cannot but know, whether as men or Christians, to be for the most part every way equal or superior to himself: how he can display with such vanity and ostentation his regal splendour so supereminently above other mortal men ; or, being a Christian, can assume such extraordinary honour and worship to himself, while the kingdom of Christ, our common king and lord, is hid to this world, and such gentilish imitation forbid in express words by himself to all his disciples. All protestants hold that Christ in his church hath left no vicegerent of his power ; but himself, without deputy, is the only head thereof governing it from heaven : how then can any Christian man derive his kingship from Christ, but with worse usurpation than the pope his headship over the church, since Christ not only hath not left the least shadow of a command for any such vicegerence from him in the state, as the pope pretends for his in the church, but hath expressly declared that such regal dominion is from the gentiles, not from him, and hath strictly charged us not to imitate them therein?

I doubt not but all ingenuous and knowing men will easily agree with me, that a free commonwealth without single person or house of lords is by far the best government, if it can be had ; but we have all this while, say they, been expecting it, and cannot yet attain it. It is true, indeed, when monarchy was dissolved, the form of a commonwealth should have forthwith been framed, aud the practice thereof immediately begun ; that the people might have soon been satisfied and delighted with the decent order, ease, and benefit

18

thereof; we had been then by this time firmly
rooted, past fear of commotions or mutations, and
now flourishing; this care of timely settling a new
government instead of the old, too much neglected,
hath been our mischief. Yet the cause thereof
may be ascribed with most reason to the frequent
disturbances, interruptions, and dissolutions, which
the parliament hath had, partly from the impatient
or disaffected people, partly from some ambitious
leaders in the army; much contrary, I believe, to
the mind and approbation of the army itself, and
their other commanders, once undeceived, or in
their own power.

Now is the opportunity, now the very season,
wherein we may obtain a free commonwealth, and
establish it for ever in the land, without difficulty
or much delay. Writs are sent out for elections,
and, which is worth observing, in the name, not
of any king, but of the keepers of our liberty, to
summon a free parliament; which then only will
indeed be free, and deserve the true honour of that
supreme title, if they preserve us a free people.
Which never parliament was more free to do,
being now called not as heretofore, by the summons
of a king, but by the voice of liberty. And if the
people, laying aside prejudice and impatience, will
seriously and calmly now consider their own good,
both religious and civil, their own liberty and the
only means thereof, as shall be here laid down
before them, and will elect their knights and
burgesses able men, and according to the just and

necessary qualifications, (which, for aught I hear, remain yet in force unrepealed, as they were formerly decreed in parliament,) men not addicted to a single person or house of lords, the work is done ; at least the foundation firmly laid of a free commonwealth, and good part also erected of the main structure. For the ground and basis of every just and free government, (since men have smarted so oft for committing all to one person,) is a general council of ablest men, chosen by the people to consult of public affairs from time to time for the common good. In this grand council must the sovereignty, not transferred, but delegated only, and as it were deposited, reside ; with this caution, they must have the forces by sea and land committed to them for preservation of the common peace and liberty ; must raise and manage the public revenue, at least with some inspectors deputed for satisfaction of the people, how it is employed ; must make or propose, as more expressly shall be said anon, civil laws, treat of commerce, peace or war with foreign nations ; and, for the carrying on some particular affairs with more secrecy and expedition, must elect, as they have already out of their own number and others, a council of state.

And, although it may seem strange at first hearing, by reason that men's minds are prepossessed with the notion of successive parliaments, I affirm that the grand or general council, being well chosen, should be perpetual : for so their business

is or may be, and ofttimes urgent ; the opportunity
of affairs gained or lost in a moment. The day of
council cannot be set as the day of a festival ; but
must be ready always to prevent or answer all
occasions. By this continuance they will become
every way skilfullest, best provided of intelligence
from abroad, best acquainted with the people at
home, and the people with them. The ship of
the commonwealth is always under sail ; they sit
at the stern, and if they steer well, what need is
there to change them, it being rather dangerous ?
Add to this, that the grand council is both foundation and main pillar of the whole state ; and to
move pillars and foundations, not faulty, cannot
be safe for the building.

I see not, therefore, how we can be advantaged
by successive and transitory parliaments ; but that
they are much likelier continually to unsettle
rather than to settle a free government, to breed
commotions, changes, novelties, and uncertainties,
to bring neglect upon present affairs and opportunities, while all minds are in suspense with expectation of a new assembly, and the assembly,
for a good space, taken up with the new settling
of itself. After which, if they find no great work
to do, they will make it, by altering or repealing
former acts, or making and multiplying new ; that
they may seem to see what their predecessors saw
not, and not to have assembled for nothing ; till
all law be lost in the multitude of clashing statutes.
But if the ambition of such as think themselves

injured that they also partake not of the government, and are impatient till they be chosen, cannot
brook the perpetuity of others chosen before them ;
or if it be feared, that long continuance of power
may corrupt sincerest men, the known expedient
is, and by some lately propounded, that annually
(or if the space be longer, so much perhaps the
better) the third part of senators may go out according to the precedence of their election, and
the like number be chosen in their places, to prevent their settling of too absolute a power, if it
should be perpetual : and this they call 'partial
'rotation.'

*　　*　　*　　*　　*　　*　　*

Having thus far shewn with what ease we may
now obtain a free commonwealth, and by it, with
as much ease, all the freedom, peace, justice,
plenty, that we can desire ; on the other side, the
difficulties, troubles, uncertainties, nay rather im-
possibilities, to enjoy these things constantly under
a monarch ; I will now proceed to show more
particularly wherein our freedom and flourishing
condition will be more ample and secure to us
under a free commonwealth than under kingship.

The whole freedom of man consists either in
spiritual or civil liberty. As for spiritual, who
can be at rest, who can enjoy anything in this
world with contentment, who hath not liberty to
serve God, and to save his own soul, according to
the best light which God hath planted in him to

that purpose, by the reading of his revealed will, and the guidance of his Holy Spirit? That this is best pleasing to God, and that the whole protestant church allows no supreme judge or rule in matters of religion, but the Scriptures; and these to be interpreted by the Scriptures themselves, which necessarily infers liberty of conscience, I have heretofore proved at large in another treatise; and might yet further, by the public declarations, confessions, and admonitions of whole churches and states, obvious in all histories since the reformation.

This liberty of conscience, which above all other things ought to be to all men dearest and most precious, no government more inclinable not to favour only, but to protect, than a free commonwealth; as being most magnanimous, most fearless, and confident of its own fair proceedings. Whereas kingship, though looking big, yet indeed most pusillanimous, full of fears, full of jealousies, startled at every umbrage, as it hath been observed of old to have ever suspected most and mistrusted them who were in most esteem for virtue and generosity of mind, so it is now known to have most in doubt and suspicion them who are most reputed to be religious. Queen Elizabeth, though herself accounted so good a protestant, so moderate, so confident of her subjects' love, would never give way so much as to presbyterian reformation in this land, though once and again besought, as Camden relates; but imprisoned and persecuted the very proposers thereof, alleging it as her mind and maxim unalterable, that such reformation would diminish regal authority.

What liberty of conscience can we then expect of others, far worse principled from the cradle, trained up and governed by popish and Spanish counsels, and on such depending hitherto for sub- sistence? Especially what can this last parliament expect, who having revived lately and published the covenant, have re-engaged themselves never to readmit episcopacy? Which no son of Charles returning but will most certainly bring back with him, if he regard the last and strictest charge of his father, 'to persevere in not the doctrine only 'but government of the church of England, not to 'neglect the speedy and effectual suppressing of 'errors and schisms;' among which he accounted presbytery one of the chief.

Or if, notwithstanding that charge of his father, he submit to the covenant, how will he keep faith to us, with disobedience to him; or regard that faith given, which must be founded on the breach of that last and solemnest paternal charge, and the reluctance, I may say the antipathy, which is in all kings, against presbyterian and independent disci- pline? For they hear the gospel speaking much of liberty; a word which monarchy and her bishops both fear and hate, but a free commonwealth both favours and promotes; and not the word only, but the thing itself. But let our governors beware in time, lest their hard measure to liberty of conscience be found the rock whereon they shipwreck themselves, as others have now done before them, in the course wherein God was directing their steerage to a free commonwealth ; and the abandoning of all those whom they call sectaries, for the detected falsehood and ambition of some, be a wilful rejection of their own chief strength and interest in the freedom of all protestant religion, under what abusive name soever calumniated.

The other part of our freedom consists in the civil rights and advancements of every person according to his merits : the enjoyment of those never more certain, and the access to these never more open, than in a free commonwealth.   Both which, in my opinion, may be best and soonest obtained, if every county in the land were made a kind of subordinate commonalty or commonwealth, and one chief town or more, according as the shire is in circuit, made cities, if they be not so called already ; where the nobility and chief gentry, from a proportionable compass of territory annexed to each city, may build houses or palaces befitting their quality ; may bear part in the government, make their own judicial laws, or use those that are, and execute them by their own elected judicatures and judges without appeal, in all things of civil government between man and man.   So they shall have justice in their own hands, law executed fully and finally in their own counties and precincts, long wished and spoken of, but never yet obtained.   They shall have none then to blame

but themselves, if it be not well administered; and
fewer laws to expect or fear from the supreme
authority ; or to those that shall be made, of any
great concernment to public liberty, they may
without much trouble in these commonalties, or
in more general assemblies called to their cities
from the whole territory on such occasions, declare
and publish their assent or dissent by deputies,
within a time limited, sent to the grand council ;
yet so as this their judgment declared shall submit to the greater number of other counties or
commonalties, and not avail them to any exemption of themselves, or refusal of agreement with
the rest, as it may in any of the United Provinces,
being sovereign within itself, ofttimes to the great
disadvantage of that union.

In these employments they may, much better
than they do now, exercise and fit themselves till
their lot fall to be chosen into the grand council,
according as their worth and merit shall be taken
notice of by the people. As for controversies that
shall happen between men of several counties,
they may repair, as they do now, to the capital
city, or any other more commodious, indifferent
place, and equal judges. And this I find to have
been practised in the old Athenian commonwealth,
reputed the first and ancientest place of civility in
all Greece ; that they had in their several cities a
peculiar, in Athens a common government ; and
their right, as it befell them, to the administration
of both.

They should have here also schools and academies at their own choice, wherein their children may be bred up in their own sight to all learning and noble education ; not in grammar only, but in all liberal arts and exercises. This would soon spread much more knowledge and civility, yea, religion, through all parts of the land, by communicating the natural heat of government and culture more distributively to all extreme parts, which now lie numb and neglected ; would soon make the whole nation more industrious, more ingenious at home, more potent, more honourable abroad. To this a free commonwealth will easily assent ; (nay, the parliament hath had already some such thing in design ;) for of all governments a commonwealth aims most to make the people flourishing, virtuous, noble, and high-spirited. Monarchs will never permit ; whose aim is to make the people wealthy indeed perhaps, and well fleeced, for their own shearing, and the supply of regal prodigality ; but otherwise softest, basest, viciousest, servilest, easiest to be kept under. And not only in fleece, but in mind also sheepishest ; and will have all the benches of judicature annexed to the throne, as a gift of royal grace that we have justice done us ; whenas nothing can be more essential to the freedom of a people, than to have the administration of justice, and all public ornaments, in their own election, and within their own bounds, without long travelling or depending upon remote places to obtain their right, or any civil accomplishment ; so it be not supreme, but subordinate to the general power and union of the whole republic.

In which happy firmness, as in the particular above-mentioned, we shall also far exceed the United Provinces, by having not as they, (to the retarding and distracting ofttimes of their counsels or urgentest occasions,) many sovereignties united in one commonwealth, but many commonwealths under one united and intrusted sovereignty. And when we have our forces by sea and land, either of a faithful army or a settled militia, in our own hands, to the firm establishing of a free commonwealth, public accounts under our own inspection, general laws and taxes, with their causes, in our own domestic suffrages, judicial laws, offices, and ornaments at home in our own ordering and administration, all distinction of lords and commoners, that may any way divide or sever the public interest, removed ; what can a perpetual senate have then wherein to grow corrupt, wherein to encroach upon us, or usurp ? Or if they do, wherein to be formidable ? Yet if all this avail not to remove the fear or envy of a perpetual sitting, it may be easily provided to change a third part of them yearly, or every two or three years, as was above mentioned : or that it be at those times in the people's choice, whether they will change them, or renew their power, as they shall find cause.

I have no more to say at present : few words will save us, well considered ; few and easy things, now seasonably done. But if the people be so affected as to prostitute religion and liberty to the vain and groundless apprehension that nothing but kingship can restore trade, not remembering the frequent plagues and pestilences that then wasted this city, such as through God's mercy we never have felt since ; and that trade flourishes nowhere more than in the free commonwealths of Italy, Germany, and the Low Countries, before their eyes at this day ; yet if trade be grown so craving and importunate through the profuse living of tradesmen that nothing can support it but the luxurious expenses of a nation upon trifles or superfluities ; so as if the people generally should betake themselves to frugality, it might prove a dangerous matter, lest tradesmen should mutiny for want of trading ; and that therefore we must forego and set to sale religion, liberty, honour, safety, all concernments divine or human, to keep up trading : if, lastly, after all this light among us, the same reason shall pass for current, to put our necks again under kingship, as was made use of by the Jews to return back to Egypt, and to the worship of their idol queen, because they falsely imagined that they then lived in more plenty and prosperity ; our condition is not sound, but rotten, both in religion and all civil prudence ; and will bring us soon, the way we are marching, to those calamities which attend always and unavoidably on luxury, all national judgments under foreign and domestic slavery : so far we shall be from mending our condition by monarchizing our government, whatever new conceit now possesses us.

However, with all hazard I have ventured what I thought my duty to speak in season, and to forewarn my country in time; wherein I doubt not but there be many wise men in all places and degrees, but am sorry the effects of wisdom are so little seen among us. Many circumstances and particulars I could have added in those things whereof I have spoken: but a few main matters now put speedily in execution will suffice to recover us, and set all right: and there will want at no time who are good at circumstances; but men who set their minds on main matters, and sufficiently urge them, in these most difficult times I find not many.

What I have spoken, is the language of that which is not called amiss 'The good old Cause:' if it seem strange to any, it will not seem more strange, I hope, than convincing to backsliders. Thus much I should perhaps have said, though I was sure I should have spoken only to trees and stones, and had none to cry to, but with the prophet, 'O earth, earth, earth!' to tell the very soil itself, what her perverse inhabitants are deaf to. Nay, though what I have spoke should happen (which thou suffer not, who didst create mankind free! nor thou next, who didst redeem us from being servants of men!) to be the last words of our expiring liberty. But I trust I shall have spoken persuasion to abundance of sensible and ingenuous men; to some, perhaps, whom God may raise from these stones to become children of reviving liberty ; and may reclaim, though they seem now choosing them a captain back for Egypt, to bethink themselves a little, and consider whither they are rushing ; to exhort this torrent also of the people not to be so impetuous, but to keep their due channel ; and at length recovering and uniting their better resolutions, now that they see already how open and unbounded the insolence and rage is of our common enemies, to stay these ruinous proceedings, justly and timely fearing to what a precipice of destruction the deluge of this epidemic madness would hurry us, through the general defection of a misguided and abused multitude.

www.ingramcontent.com/pod-product-compliance
Lightning Source LLC
Chambersburg PA
CBHW030627030726
47497CB00006B/1675